SACRED
SEVENTH

AURELIUS
PUBLISHING

Published by Aurelius Publishing

aurelius.com.au
peter@aurelius.com.au

First printed: January 2026

Cover design by Jess Chaplin
Typeset by Jess Chaplin

Paperback ISBN: 978-0-6488717-1-2
Digital Online epub ISBN: 978-0-6488717-2-9

SACRED SEVENTH

PETER BELL

Mum and Chris

*This story took the better part of three years to write,
and in that time you both left this world.*

*There were days I wanted to walk away from the page
altogether, but the memory of your love, kindness and
fierce support kept pulling me back.*

I finished this book for you, and because of you.

*May it stand as a small part of your legacy
and a thank you for everything you gave me.*

You will never be forgotten and are missed dearly.

CARMEL MARY BELL 1952–2025

CHRISTOPHER JOHN BOYLE 1989–2023

CONTENTS

CHAPTER 1 - Closed 1

CHAPTER 2 - Celebrations 4

CHAPTER 3 - Craig's Creative Accounting 12

CHAPTER 4 - Hazel's Last Twenty Thousand 18

CHAPTER 5 - The Honeymoon Period 23

CHAPTER 6 - Pressure Builds 29

CHAPTER 7 - Bitter Disappointment 35

CHAPTER 8 - When Good People Break 41

CHAPTER 9 - The Woman Who Faints 47

CHAPTER 10 - The Drop 49

CHAPTER 11 - The Crew in the Zoo 53

CHAPTER 12 - The Sacred Pact 60

CHAPTER 13 - The Calls 68

CHAPTER 14 - Donnelly's Bet 72

CHAPTER 15 - Race 7 76

CHAPTER 16 - Counting the Cost 81

CHAPTER 17 - Locking Up 89

CHAPTER 18 - The Aftermath 95

CHAPTER 19 - The Birthday Confession 102

CHAPTER 20 - The Unexpected Call 109

CHAPTER 21 - What Really Matters 114

CHAPTER 22 - Connection 118

CHAPTER 23 - New Life 131

CHAPTER 24 - Good Company 138

CHAPTER 1

CLOSED

Brisbane, late 1992

Michael Whelan lay in darkness in his southside Brisbane bedroom. Nothing stirred. A lone streetlight outside cast a dim glow through the blinds. His mind cycled through every misstep that had brought him to this unfamiliar edge.

Beside him, his wife Daniela breathed softly. Did she still dream of hallways echoing with laughter, or had disappointment pulled her into the same uneasy undercurrent of regret and yearning that tugged at him?

That morning, he kissed Daniela goodbye as she left for work. He told her he was working from home that day. Mid-morning, he drove to Aspley. His heart thundered, sweat trickling down his spine as he stared at the duffle bag on the passenger seat. Inside: a balaclava, a crowbar, cable ties and a shotgun wrapped in tattered cloth.

Michael Whelan, a well-educated office professional, had never imagined himself here. The law saw him as a clean slate, with only a few traffic offences. He had always viewed robbers as reckless or hopeless, not men like him.

He had chosen his target carefully. Not a bank, not a petrol station, too many cameras; he needed a target slow to adopt new security measures. A TAB outlet in Aspley, on Brisbane's northside, had caught his attention. A safe distance from his Mt Gravatt home. No reinforced screens, a single cashier, and older-style security cameras mounted high and poorly angled. There would be an alarm, perhaps a delay safe, but he was ready to risk what little he had left.

He parked with deliberate caution, neither too close nor too far. His fingers drummed against the steering wheel, each tap fuelled by dread as anxious questions crowded his mind. From the car, he could see the entrance and the constant shuffle of patrons.

The late morning heat radiated from the pavement. A sleek black Mercedes pulled into the car park. The driver emerged, polished in a Hilfiger shirt with a sharp jawline. Michael sneered. The man reminded him of his brother-in-law, Leo Jr, the golden boy in the extended family. Three children, a holiday house at the coast and a big boat, "Pity he's still a wanker," Michael muttered while slamming his elbow into the car door.

He snapped up the duffle bag and yanked it open. The mental countdown began.

Five. Four. Three. Two. One.

He tugged the balaclava over his head, stepped from the car and slung the bag over his shoulder, one hand gripping the hidden shotgun.

Once inside, he flipped the sign from OPEN to CLOSED and wedged the crowbar between the door handles.

"Hands up. No one move. No heroes and everyone walks away."

The shotgun was shaking in his grasp. Then he saw her, the cashier. An older woman. Her eyes, wide open, staring straight down the barrel.

A hush swept through the room.

Michael Whelan faltered. His thoughts fractured, as an overwhelming tide of self-loathing and doubt surged through him.

"Fuck me," he mumbled.

CHAPTER 2

CELEBRATIONS

Brisbane, 1955-1988 and late 1992

Hazel Andrews had always believed fear didn't need proof. Proof was for accountants and men like her now-departed husband.

Fear didn't wait for any of that. Fear turned up in the body first and argued its case afterwards. Sometimes it whispered. Sometimes it crawled up the back of your neck and sat there for years. And sometimes, she was discovering, it simply walked in one ordinary day and pointed a shotgun at your chest.

The man in the balaclava stood three metres from her, breathing hard through the knitted wool. The gun looked foreign in his grasp. His hands weren't steady, not properly. Anyone else might have seen that nervous tremor and felt reassured.

Hazel knew better. Men like that often did their stupidest thing when they were trying to prove they weren't scared.

"Hands up. No one move. No heroes and everyone walks away."

His voice cracked halfway through the sentence. If he heard it, he gave no visible sign to Hazel. Adrenaline had a way of making people deaf to themselves.

Hazel's fingers uncurled from the betting slips she'd been tallying. Paper fanned onto the counter, sliding across the laminate. Someone behind her gave a small, shocked sound and smothered it. Outside, traffic hummed along Gympie Road as if the situation inside hadn't yet solidified.

Her shoulders lifted, slow and deliberate. She raised her hands where he could see them.

Her attention went where it always did in a crisis: not to the weapon, but to the faces.

The man in the nice shirt by the form guide board froze mid-page turn, lips parted. The pale woman in the summery blouse clutched her handbag strap tightly. A bloke in a singlet near the back had his mouth set, eyes already fixated on the robber.

Hazel's gaze found her own outline in the scratched Perspex screen. A small woman in a green TAB polo, silver hair scraped back, glasses on a chain, expression somewhere between wary and tired.

Once, there'd been a different kind of image she portrayed.

1955, Brisbane. The Johnstone Gallery in Bowen Hills smelled of solvent paint and opportunity.

Hazel Clarke stood just inside the entrance, pretending to read the small catalogue in her hands. She'd spent all morning convincing herself she had the right to be there. Ten minutes in the room, and she was already waiting for someone to tap her shoulder and ask who had let her in.

Guests drifted past in pairs and clusters. Pearls, hats and

summer fabrics. Murmured opinions, careful laughter, the tinkle of glassware. Down the central wall her canvases hung between bigger, brasher work.

"Excuse me, are you Hazel Clarke?"

The voice came from just behind her right shoulder, smooth and clear. Hazel turned.

The woman facing her wore a simple dark dress with a strand of pearls that somehow made the whole room look underdressed. Her name badge read *Jennifer*. Her gaze was level, unhurried, the kind of attention Hazel wasn't used to being on the receiving end of.

"Yes," Hazel managed. "That's me."

"I'm very glad." Jennifer's eyes flicked to the wall. "Your work is striking. There's a tension in it that stays with you."

Hazel glanced instinctively at her nearest canvas: a bruised sky, storm-heavy water, a single dark shape on a headland, caught between leaving and staying.

"Plenty of tension in the person who painted it, also," she said.

Jennifer smiled, not the standard dismissive smile people gave when they didn't want to argue. This one had weight.

"Art doesn't belong to deserving," she said. "It belongs to honesty. And you are telling the truth, even when it's not pretty. That's rarer than you think."

"I'll spend some more time with the pieces," Jennifer added. "But I already know one of them is coming home with me."

The words *home with me* landed hard. Hazel had prepared for indifference, even mockery. Not this. Someone claiming her work because it mattered to them.

When she finally flopped into a chair behind a display wall, her legs were shaking. From there she watched people tilt their heads in front of her canvases and debate their merits in low voices. It felt, briefly, like she existed.

"Pardon me. May I join you?"

The man standing there didn't look like he belonged in an art gallery. His suit was ordinary in a well-meaning way, his tie slightly crooked, his hair more sensible than stylish. He held himself like someone more used to committee rooms than champagne.

"You can," Hazel said. "But I may not be sparkling company."

He smiled and offered his hand.

"Jim Andrews," he said. "And you must be the talented Miss Clarke."

"Talented?" Hazel looked down at the floorboards. "Art's fickle. Admired one minute, ignored the next."

"So is life," he said, settling beside her. "But some things endure. I hope your work is one of them."

They talked until staff began stacking glasses and murmuring about closing. Jim asked clear, unpatronising questions about her process. He listened when she answered, really listened, brows drawn, occasional little nods as if he were filing each answer somewhere useful.

When he finally stood to leave, he took a napkin from the nearest tray, pulled a pen from his pocket, and scribbled on the paper.

"If you're ever in the city during the week," he said, sliding the napkin towards her, "come by this café. I'm there most mornings around eight. We can argue some more about what deserves to last."

Hazel took the napkin. The ink was already smudging slightly where he'd pressed hard.

"I might," she said.

She tucked it into her handbag later that night. Not out of any grand romantic conviction, she wasn't foolish enough for that. Out of curiosity. And out of the quiet, unfamiliar pleasure of having been seen.

A cough snapped her back to the TAB.

The pale woman near the trifecta board cleared her throat. The man in the balaclava jerked towards the sound, like a skittish horse avoiding a pesky blow fly.

"Don't move," he barked, louder this time.

Hazel's breath tightened. Years of painting had trained her to notice tiny shifts in light and shape. Years of being married to Jim had trained her to notice tiny shifts in men right before they did something reckless.

The TV above the robber's shoulder flicked between silent ads. Banking. Cars. Politicians shaking hands. For a heartbeat the image froze on a younger Bob Hawke during Australia's Bicentennial year, in a garish blazer, microphone in hand, selling optimism to a racing crowd.

Hazel almost snorted. Rogues came in all forms. Some sold dreams, some sold schemes. Some turned up with a shotgun.

The time warp on TV took her back to a time when celebrations were regular.

1988, Brisbane. The lift doors to the sixteenth-floor function room opened and pushed Hazel and Jim into a wall of noise.

Applause rolled across the carpet. Someone wolf-whistled. A band in the corner stumbled halfway through a sax solo as the room pivoted towards Jim.

"This is too much," Hazel said, half-laughing, half-wincing.

"It's not enough," Jim replied, already straightening his tie, smoothing his hair with the flat of his hand. "Nearly forty years of service and they still made me bring my own cake."

"They'll reimburse the cake," Hazel said. "Provided your form finds the right in-tray."

"You know what I mean." Jim grinned, the showman spark already in his eyes.

He let go of her hand to listen to formalities. The boss said a few words about loyalty and dedication. Jim shook his hand, nodded at the right places, then stepped forward.

"Most of you know I started in this department when we still had ink wells on the desks," he began. The crowd laughed obligingly. "We've seen typewriters give way to computers, paper ledgers give way to screens, and afternoon smoko give way to whatever this," he lifted his champagne flute, "is supposed to be."

More laughter. Hazel watched him from their table near the front, pride and unease doing their usual wrestle in her chest. He was good at this. Too good.

"What doesn't change," Jim went on, "is my desire to build something that matters. To leave a little more than we found."

His eyes found her in the crowd and softened for a fraction of a second.

"I haven't always got that balance right," he said. "But I've had someone beside me who believed I could. Hazel, love, raise your hand."

Heat rushed into her face. The room clapped. Jim waited until the noise died.

"This woman held our life together so I could chase opportunities," he said. "She backed every hunch, smiled through every late night. Now it's time for me to back one of hers as she spends more time dedicated to her art."

Curious looks rippled through the room.

"And as some of you already know," Jim continued, "I've taken a stake in a new venture … a TAB, up in Aspley. Well, with the help of a close friend and expert in the numbers game." He gestured towards a man at the bar.

Hazel followed his gesture. Craig stood there in an immaculate suit, glass in hand.

After the formalities subsided, Jim leaned across the half-eaten desserts where Hazel was now seated and took her hand.

"This is it," he said. "Our last big move. Craig's set it up through a trust, very clever arrangement. We buy in cheap and sell it down the track to maximise the upside."

Hazel listened. She understood almost none of the jargon and all of the tone.

"How much of the house is in it?" she asked quietly.

"Not the house," he said, too quickly. "Just … you know. Some up-front cash equity. It's safe, love. I wouldn't do it otherwise."

She held his gaze. She'd watched him work a room all evening, watched the way the story of his career became smoother each time he told it. Underneath all the polish, there was the same young man who'd once sat in a quiet café and asked her about colour and light until she forgot to be shy. She still believed in that young man.

She didn't entirely trust the man beside him at the bar.

"Promise me," she said. "Five years. Then we walk away. No matter what Craig says. We don't chase it past that."

Jim's smile faltered for the first time that night.

"It won't come to that," he said, then caught himself and adjusted. "But alright. Five years. You have my word."

He raised his glass.

"To our future," he said. "Five years from now, we'll have our pick of horizons."

Hazel clinked her flute against his. The band roared into another song, laughter rose, cameras flashed. On the outside it was a celebration.

But inside, something cold stirred deep down inside Hazel Andrews.

In the Aspley TAB, four years later, that cold thing felt like a stone.

Hazel's glance dropped to the counter, to the dull metal of the till. Behind it, hidden from Craig, from the bank manager, from every well-meaning relative, from this jumpy idiot in a balaclava, lay the last of her safety, folded notes and the tiny hope that she could still claw something back.

She swallowed, mouth dry. The gun's black circles hadn't shifted.

This was what all those retirement dreams had bought her: a fading little shop with a busted alarm, an accountant who'd circled her like a vulture, and now a stranger deciding whether today was the day everyone's luck ended.

She drew a slow breath, willing her voice to behave.

"Alright, love," she said to the robber, and her own steadiness surprised her. "Let's not do anything stupid today."

The room tightened. Somewhere beneath the stone in her chest, the old artist who still lived in her bones framed the scene out of habit, four people, one gun, and several bad decisions all converging in a strip-lit box on Gympie Road.

However this picture turned out, she intended to be alive to see it.

CHAPTER 3

CRAIG'S CREATIVE ACCOUNTING

Brisbane, late 1992 and earlier that year

The balaclava dipped as the shotgun shifted a fraction closer.

Hazel could see the man's eyes now, dark through the wool, unfocused in that particular way people got when fear was driving faster than sense. Sweat gathered under the strip of skin visible between mask and collar. His finger twitched near the trigger.

"Open the register," he said. "Now."

The room seemed to tilt. Behind him, the TAB screens cycled through odds and fluctuations. A multitude of numbers that only meant something to a select few. Hazel's fingers curled around the edge of the counter to stop her tremor.

It wasn't just the gun. It wasn't just the robber. It was that same feeling.

Cornered again. Men holding all the power; her left to sweep up the mess.

An old kitchen in Geebung rose up in her mind.

Hazel sat at her sister's table, a pile of envelopes between them.

Kathryn's linoleum floor had started to curl at the edges. There were faint outlines where old rugs had once been. Tiny ants wandered over the pile of paperwork, scavenging for any stale food remnants.

In the middle of it all sat a chipped teapot and a plate of dry biscuits better suited to a dog.

Kathryn nudged the plate towards her sister. "You really should eat something, lovey. Might help you."

Hazel picked up a biscuit. Her veined hands shook as she snapped it in half. Crumbs scattered onto the lace doily like little fragments of something that used to be whole.

"I'm too old for this stress, Kath," she said, staring at the crumbs. "Too tired. How could Jim do this to me?"

"You can't blame yourself," Kathryn replied, voice soft but firm. "You did what all of us did. That's how it is. Men handle the money. I let Mervyn do the same."

Hazel snorted, a rough little sound. "I wouldn't compare Mervyn with Jim. At least your Mervyn didn't leave you indebted to half of Brisbane when he passed on. Can't say the same for my 'not' dearly departed."

The last words came out brittle. Tears welled.

She stared into her tea. Leaves drifted in slow spirals, like they were going somewhere she no longer could.

Kathryn reached across and laid a calming hand over Hazel's fingers.

"God help me, Kath," Hazel whispered.

"All the savings gone," she said. "His super bled dry. I worked my whole life as an artist and I'm one bill away from your couch for life."

"You come here as long as you need," Kathryn said simply. "We'll manage. But I still say you talk to Craig. He's been your accountant since forever. He'll have to explain this mess."

Hazel's mouth tightened. "Craig explains everything in a way that just happens to end in his invoice being paid."

"He's clever with numbers," Kathryn said. "You need clever right now."

"I need honest," Hazel muttered. "Preferably in writing."

She looked again at the envelopes. Somewhere in there was Craig's details.

"Fine," she said. "I'll go see him. But I want answers, not a condescending performance."

Inside the TAB, the robber shifted his stance.

"Did you hear me?" he snapped. "Open it."

Hazel forced herself to nod, fingers creeping toward the keypad.

Just as her fingertips prepared to hit CASH OUT, a different kind of fear flared, the memory of the last time she'd met with Craig.

Visiting Craig's office in the CBD always made Hazel feel inferior.

Too many certificates on the walls, all those gold seals and heavy frames insisting he knew best. A view over the river that said *success* even if Hazel now knew how thin the foundations underneath could be.

"Hazel," Craig said, rising as she stepped in. "Please. Have a seat."

He looked much the same as he had at Jim's retirement funeral: hair tidier than his conscience, glasses halfway down his nose, tie that had seen better years. His smile rehearsed. His authenticity was like a motel's 'genuine Monet' print; technically there, but nobody was fooled.

Hazel didn't sit. She closed the door behind her and stayed standing, handbag clutched like armour.

"Save it, Craig," she said. "I'm not here for pleasantries."

He blinked, then let the smile dim a fraction. "Alright. Straight to business." He gestured at the chair again. "Please. You'll be more comfortable."

Reluctantly, she sat. Not because he told her to, but because her knees had started complaining about righteous standoffs some years ago.

He slid a manila folder across the desk.

"I've been going through Jim's affairs in more detail, as you requested," he said. "There are … complexities."

"My life seems full of those lately," Hazel shot back. "Start with the basics. Where has all the money gone, Craig?"

He cleared his throat.

"Some of the investments Jim made in the last few years were high-risk," Craig said. "I set up the structures; he chased the returns."

"Don't you dare put this all on him," Hazel snapped. "What about our superannuation? What will happen to the TAB?"

"Well, the TAB, that's in a discretionary trust. On paper, very sophisticated. In practice, it means the business and its debts are handcuffed together."

"In English, Craig."

"If you try to hang on, they can take the lot," he said. "If you cooperate with a sale I arrange, we can clear most of the debt and avoid court."

She leaned forward.

"And who would I be selling to Craig?" she asked. "People in your circles? Opportunists sniffing around for a bargain? Crooks?"

Craig bristled. "That's unfair. I've been nothing but loyal to you and Jim for over thirty years."

"Spare me," she said. "Working at the TAB has taught me how this goes. You only ever slither in when there's something in it for you."

His eyes hardened.

"Hazel, listen to me," he said. "You are a widow in her sixties with limited income. The banks don't care about the years you spent supporting Jim and painting art pieces for charities. If you dig your heels in, they'll force a sale and take everything they can. I'm offering you a way to walk away with something."

"And that," she said slowly, "is assuming your mysterious buyers are the saints you claim."

"They're investors," Craig said. "They understand risk. They understand the horse racing industry. They can turn the business around."

"And pay you to oversee the lot no doubt?"

He didn't bother denying it.

"I can't change what's happened," he said. "But I can make sure it doesn't get worse. You sign these," he tapped the folder, "and we can wrap this up."

Hazel looked at the forms. Her name was already printed in the spaces, waiting for her shaky signature to make it all official.

She remembered Jim. She recalled all the nights she'd closed up the TAB, counting out notes in the harsh light, trusting that somewhere in the tangle of trusts and loans there was still something that belonged to her.

"Go frig yourself, Craig," she said quietly.

His mouth dropped open. "Hazel …"

"I'll find my own way to deal with the mess Jim left," she said. "Without handing you the keys."

In the Aspley TAB, Hazel was snapped back to her current reality.

"I said open it, lady. For fuck's sake."

Hazel pushed the key with a finger that felt like it belonged to someone else. The till drawer sprang open with a metallic clatter.

She looked at the man with the shotgun, at the tremor in the barrel and the panic tightening around his eyes.

"I'll get you what you want," she said, voice low, controlled. "Just don't point that thing at anyone's head."

Her hands moved. The till sang, notes rustled and coins clattered.

If she survived, nobody else would hold the cards over her again – not a gunman, not an accountant, not even Jim's ghost.

CHAPTER 4

HAZEL'S LAST TWENTY THOUSAND

Brisbane, late 1992

The nylon bag sat on the shelf beneath the counter, right under Hazel's knees, etched in her awareness like a live wire.

Above the counter, the duffle bag gaped waiting to be fed. The man with the shotgun, she didn't know his name yet, jerked his chin towards the till.

"Hurry up," he said. "All of it."

Hazel's fingers lifted notes from the drawer, feeding them into the bag. Rubber bands snapped against her skin. She'd done this end-of-day ritual more times than she could count, but never under duress.

Each time she dipped for another handful, her eyes strayed, quick and involuntary to check on the faded nylon bag.

Inside, wrapped in bank envelopes, was everything she had left that Craig didn't know about.

Twenty thousand. Her last reserve.

The recollection snapped her back to that morning, to the cold, bright lobby of the Queen Street Commonwealth Bank branch.

Earlier that day, the glass doors hissed shut behind her, and the bank's air-conditioning welcomed her inside.

Clean lines. White tiles. Posters of smiling couples outside brand-new homes. Young staff in crisp shirts and name badges, moving like they'd rehearsed the choreography.

Hazel adjusted the strap of her old handbag, the frayed edge biting into her shoulder. A schoolboy in uniform bobbed his head to his Walkman beside her in the queue.

Hazel admired her comfortable open-air shoes while concentrating on breathing.

When her turn came, she stepped to the counter. A girl with the name tag *Kylie* appeared on the other side. Her ponytail slicked tight and an angelic face that Hazel might have once replicated on a sketchbook page.

"Good morning," Kylie chirped. "How can we help you today?"

Hazel slid the withdrawal slip across. The ink on the numbers had blotted where her hand had been sweating.

"I'd like to withdraw twenty thousand dollars," she said, keeping her voice low, as if the amount might attract opportunists.

Kylie's smile flickered. "Twenty thousand?"

"Yes."

"From your savings account, Mrs … Andrews?" Her fingers danced over the keyboard. She glanced at the screen; her eyes tightened. "That's … most of what's left in this one."

"I'm aware," Hazel said, the words coming out tighter than she'd intended. "That's why I'm here."

"Of course." Kylie slid a second form towards her. "If you could sign here as well, I'll just get the manager's authorisation."

Hazel signed. The pen felt heavier than it had any right to.

Kylie reappeared with the manager in tow.

"Holiday plans, Mrs Andrews?" he asked, voice smooth with the usual assumptions.

Holiday. The word nearly made her laugh.

"No," she said. "I've got … commitments."

They counted the money in neat stacks, notes crisp enough to rasp as they slid them together. Kylie banded them, tucked the bundles into a thick envelope and pushed them across.

"Twenty thousand," she said. "All there. Would you like a balance printout as well?"

"No, thank you," Hazel replied.

She swept them into a nylon bag and pulled the zip closed before anyone in the queue could tilt their head and get curious.

"Have a lovely day, madam," Kylie said. "And thank you for banking with Commonwealth."

Hazel managed a nod and walked out.

She rode the bus north with the nylon bag pinned to her ribs, every hiss of the doors sounding like a threat.

The bus rattled through half-familiar suburbs and past old corner shops now shadowed by big-box stores.

When she arrived, the TAB welcomed her with its usual smell of stale cigarette smoke and disinfectant. The carpet told the story better than any ledger; old gum mashed flat, brown blooms from spilled coffee and a suspicious patch near the TV she'd chosen never to investigate.

Hazel flicked the main switch. The fluorescents coughed themselves awake, buzzing like they resented the effort.

Behind the counter, she slid the nylon bag onto the shelf where she usually kept her own things. It felt wrong leaving it there, but she couldn't exactly chain it to her wrist all day.

She crouched, nudged the bag back, tucking it behind a dusty ream of receipt paper and a box of dead pens. Still too exposed.

Still felt like she'd left her soul on the floor.

That was when she noticed the alarm panel.

The plastic cover wore a crack through the middle. A couple of wires hung loose where the electrician had left them, bright innards on show. She'd meant to get someone back to fix it. Then the invoice for the emergency roof repairs had landed, and the letter from the ATO.

'It'll be fine,' she'd told herself. Who'd bother robbing a fading suburban TAB on Gympie Road?

Even safety had become a luxury item now. One more thing she couldn't afford.

Hazel straightened and pushed the unease aside with the comfort of routine. Float the till. Count the petty cash. Unlock the doors. Make some crack to the first regular about doing his backside again. The work might be tedious, but it was still the one place she knew what she was doing.

She had no idea that, by lunchtime, she'd be wishing she'd hidden the money in the toilets instead.

In the present, with a shotgun in the room, that wish provided no value.

"Faster," the robber said. His voice was starting to fray at the edges. "Come on."

Hazel swept the last bundles of notes into the duffle. Her movements stayed brisk; panic wouldn't help anyone. The till drawer yawned mostly empty, a few coins rolling in their slots.

Behind them, the screens kept doing their oblivious dance. The three punters remained unmoved.

"That's it," she said. "You've cleaned me out."

Even if it wasn't the whole truth.

CHAPTER 5

THE HONEYMOON PERIOD

Brisbane, late 1992 and 1988-1990

The duffle bag waited on the counter.

He had pictured this scene in his head for weeks. In none of those versions had the cashier been a small, elderly woman in a faded polo; but so far no one was hurt, no one had challenged him, and no one had triggered an alarm.

Over his shoulder, one of the screens switched to a grainy clip: fireworks bursting over the Brisbane River, neon reflected in black water, crowds pressed together along the banks.

For a moment, the TAB disappeared from his mind's eye. The gun, the duffle bag, the elderly lady – all of it slid out of focus, replaced by a different counter. A younger version of himself who still believed that dreams could manifest in reality.

On most Brisbane afternoons in 1988, the humid air wasn't the only thing making Michael Whelan hot and bothered. His local Fortitude Valley café was a regular haunt. He told his work colleagues it was the choice of places for a caffeine fix near the office, but he was only fooling himself.

Behind the counter worked a young lady with dark curls and an aura that suggested Brisbane was not yet ready for beauty of such magnitude.

"Good morning. What will it be today?" she asked.

Her voice wasn't tried on in the typical, fake hospitality way. It was genuine, like she actually cared about the answer.

Michael cleared his throat, suddenly aware of the sweat mark creeping down his collar. "Just a coffee, thanks."

"Cool. Well, that narrows it down for me," she said, mouth quirking. "Flat white? Capp? Long black?"

"Flat white," he said. "One sugar. Sorry. Yeah. Flat white, one sugar."

"Coming right up." She gave him a quick, bright smile, as if he'd passed checkpoint one and she could move him through to the next round.

He took his usual seat by the window and tried not to stare at her reflection in the glass.

After that, he started planning his morning café visits to align with her predictable shift patterns.

Weeks went by. Same order, same banter. One Wednesday, she set his cup down and didn't drift away.

"I've noticed you here a lot lately," she said, giving him a more deliberate once-over.

His stomach gave a ridiculous little lurch. "Yeah. I suppose I can't resist the coffee here … and the company."

The line left his mouth before he could run quality control on it. He braced for the flinch, the eyeroll, the polite step back.

Instead, her smile spread. "Smooth."

"Terrible, actually," he said quickly. "Let me try again before you ban me. Would you … like to get out of here sometime? Grab a meal? Somewhere that doesn't pay you to listen to idiots like me?"

She tilted her head, weighing him up. For a moment he felt like a house at an open-home – lights on, doors wide, waiting to see if anyone put in an offer.

"I'd like that," she said. No drama. Just 'yes'.

Something inside his chest slid into a new position and locked there.

Back in the TAB, precious time was now passing. Michael was aware that the guy in the Hilfiger shirt by the door was tracking his every move, as if he were mentally drafting a report. At the same time, the scruffy bloke at the back appeared to be calmly critiquing his robbery performance.

You're doing this for her, Michael told himself. For Daniela. For whatever started at that café counter and refused to let go.

Their first date pushed up in his mind whether he invited it or not.

World Expo '88 had turned Brisbane into somewhere else for a while. Louder. Brighter. Like the city had stolen someone else's formal attire and was enjoying how it looked on them.

They'd picked a Friday night. Both finished work early and caught the 444 bus in. The closer they got to South Brisbane, the more the atmosphere changed – music leaking over the river, pockets of foreign languages, the constant churn of generators and rides.

"Right," Daniela said at the gates, already steering. "Italian Pavilion first."

Michael fiddled with the paper wristband the volunteer had snapped around his arm. "So this Italian Pavilion is better than the Irish one, is it?"

"You'll see, Irishman." She nudged his shoulder, eyes sparking. "Then you'll thank me for introducing you to real culture."

Inside, the Italian Pavilion was a wall of warmth and noise – garlic and olive oil hanging in the air, conversations layered over each other, Napoli posters and black-and-white village photos stacked on the walls. Women who could have been someone's nonna handed out samples with the force of an ultimatum.

Daniela moved through it like she'd been born there, talking the whole time.

"This," she said, holding a pizza slice under his nose, "is proper pizza. Thin base, fresh ingredients. Not that frozen rubbish with half a supermarket dumped on top."

He took a bite, tried not to immediately look converted. "Not bad."

"Not bad?" She planted a hand on her hip. "Admit it. Italians own food, art and culture. It's just facts."

"Alright, alright." He lifted both hands. "It's great. You win this round. But wait till you see the Irish Pavilion. I'll show you how we dance."

"Leprechauns and shamrocks?" she said. "I'm bracing myself."

The Irish Pavilion, when they finally found it, was … less impressive. A few flags. Faded posters. A bloke with a tin whistle who looked like he'd been given the wrong shift and no way out.

Michael glanced at her. She was biting her lip, clearly trying not to laugh.

"Okay," he said. "You win this time, Italian princess. Let's not make a habit of it, yeah?"

She slid her fingers through his. "No promises."

They ended up in one of the outdoor beer gardens as the sun dropped. A cover band murdered 80s pop under strings of fairy lights. Plastic cups stuck slightly to the tables. The river glittered in a show-off kind of way.

"How about a drink and a dance, twinkle-toes?" she said.

"Sounds like a plan," he replied. "West Coast Cooler for you. Guinness for me."

He shouldered through the crowd to the bar, ordered, then turned back to find her watching him over the heads of strangers. When he reached the table, their eyes met over the rims of their drinks.

"To Expo," he said.

"To us," she countered.

They tapped plastic. For a few seconds, the music and voices blurred and the shed-dressed city felt like theirs.

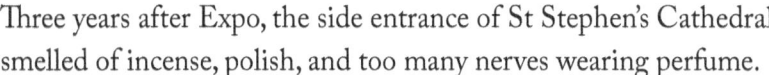

Three years after Expo, the side entrance of St Stephen's Cathedral smelled of incense, polish, and too many nerves wearing perfume.

Michael stood in the strip of shade near Ann Street, fiddling with the knot of the Hugo Boss tie Daniela had insisted on. It had been on sale, but it still felt like he had a week's wages looped around his neck.

"The flower sits perfect, stop pulling at things," Maeve said, fussing with his lapel. His mother had that look she got at graduations and funerals – half proud, half terrified of crying in public.

Inside the cathedral, ivy and pale roses ran along the pew ends like a magazine spread only slightly downgraded for budget. Stone walls threw every sound back – organ, footsteps, whispered assessments from the Bianchi cousins who'd flown in.

Michael stood at the front, sweating under the jacket, watching the doors.

Then the music changed. People stood. Maeve's hand flew to her mouth. Daniela came down the aisle on her father's arm, dress catching the light, veil soft around her face. Her eyes found him and everything else faded out.

"Well, hello there, spunky man," she mouthed.

He laughed under his breath, shoulders dropping a fraction. When she reached him, he took her hand and lifted it slightly.

He said the words the priest prompted – richer, poorer, sickness, health – and meant every single one. He couldn't give her a family estate or a family business or a holiday house at the coast, but he could give her hard work, loyalty, and the certainty that he'd stand between her and anything life threw.

"I'll take care of you," he'd told her later, when they stumbled out into the afternoon light with rice in their hair and lipstick on his cheek.

She'd smiled like that was a given. "I know," she'd said. "We'll take care of each other."

CHAPTER 6

PRESSURE BUILDS

Brisbane, late 1992 and early 1992

M ichael had been in the TAB now for ten minutes.
"Is that all?" he heard himself say. His voice came out rough.
"That's the till," she said. "Like you asked."

Around them, the TAB played its usual song – monotone commentary, fridge rattle, the slow tick of the clock above the TV. On one screen, an ad cut in. A bloke in a button-up short-sleeve shirt at a drafting table, tracing neat lines across a house plan for a young family looking to build a new home.

The ad yanked him backwards in time as the monotonous TAB hum turned into lively office murmurs.

Fortitude Valley's urban renewal precinct was starting to buzz in early 1992.

In Michael's converted industrial warehouse office, phones rang, and people laughed loudly near the kitchenette. A radio crackled as INXS played under the churn of voices. The office air had that usual mix – paper, toner, overheated brains pushing deadlines around.

Michael hunched over his drawing board, sleeves rolled, plans fanned out. He was halfway through a load-bearing wall detail, pencil skating along a ruler, when his desk phone trilled.

"Hi Michael, I've got Daniela on the phone for you," Diana called from reception.

"Thanks, Di. Put her through."

He rolled his shoulders, trying to shake out the tightness between his shoulder blades. Outside the window the river glared.

"Hey, love," he said, putting a smile into his voice for her benefit. "What's up?"

"Hi, Mikey. Can you talk?"

Her voice wasn't its usual brisk café style. Softer. Pensive. Threads of something in it that delivered instant presence of mind – not quite fear, not quite hope.

"Yeah," he said. "Everything alright?"

A small pause. "I think so. I think … I may be pregnant."

He shot upright. The chair slapped back into the partition.

"Are you serious?" His voice came out too loud; he hunched over the phone, lowering it. "Dani, that's … that's huge."

"My period's late," she continued. "It's never late. I've been nauseous for two weeks, feel like throwing up every time I look at a cappuccino …"

His office slipped out of focus. Site meetings, beam sizes, budget arguments; all of it slid to the edge of his awareness. The clinic's brochures flashed through his head, diagrams of reproductive systems, confusing words. Months of appointments and 'we'll review your case' in polite voices.

Now this.

"Do you have a test there?" he asked.

Silence pushed down the line. He could almost see her, one hand gripping the edge of the café counter, the other wrapped around a chemist bag.

"I do," she said at last. "But I'm scared to use it. I don't want to … build myself up again. It just feels different this time. I can't explain it."

Her voice wobbled on the last few words; he noticed the tiny crack.

"I get it," he said, pressing his palm into his forehead hard enough to leave a mark. "I'm nervous too. But we need to know, Dani. We can't hang in this halfway place."

"I'll shut the office door for five minutes and do it now," she whispered. "I'll call you as soon as possible."

"Of course." His throat had gone dry. "You've got this."

She tried to laugh. "We've got this, Irishman."

The line clicked dead.

He put the receiver down carefully, as if dropping it might shatter whatever slim chance they'd been handed. For a moment, he just stared at the phone, hand hovering near it, like it might ring of its own accord if he willed it hard enough.

Pictures flooded his brain: a tiny onesie pegged on their washing line, a kid perched on his shoulders at the Ekka, someone with her dark eyes and his lopsided grin learning to kick a footy in the park.

His pulse thudded in his throat. Fifteen minutes had passed when the phone finally buzzed; he snatched it so fast the coiled plastic handset cord struggled to keep up.

"Dani?"

"It's me," she said. The words were barely there.

"What did it say?"

"It's … it's negative." The sentence broke in the middle. "I'm sorry. I really thought … my body felt different. I feel like an idiot."

Air left his lungs in a rush.

"Oh, Dani," he said. His voice scraped. "I'm so sorry."

"It's okay," she said automatically, but he could hear it wasn't. "I know we said we wouldn't let ourselves get carried away, but it's hard not to. I thought … maybe this time."

He tipped his head back, staring up at the ceiling.

"We've done everything they've asked," he said, the words rough. "But we still keep coming home empty."

She was quiet a moment. "It's cruel," she said at last.

He leaned forward, elbows digging into the board until the edge bit his skin. "You're the strongest person I know," he said. "However many times it takes, I'm not going anywhere."

"Thank you," she whispered. "I love you."

"I love you too."

The line went quiet.

He set the phone down slower this time. He placed his forehead in both hands. The numbers on the drawing in front of him might as well have been a language meant for somebody else's life.

He stayed like that for a long beat, listening to the office move on around him, unaware.

Pressure wasn't just a feeling. It had a décor.

For him, it looked like Casa Bianchi.

The little southside house had been scrubbed within an inch

of its existence. Daniela had dragged the dining table out to full extension, laid crisp white cloths, lined up every bit of matching crockery they owned and some they'd borrowed. Fresh flowers ran down the centre. Meat roasted low in the oven. Her nonna's sauce simmered on the stove, filling every corner with garlic, tomatoes, and history.

By the time everyone arrived for Sunday lunch, the place resembled an advertisement for 'migrant family makes good'.

"Welcome to Casa Bianchi," Leo Jr announced, already at the head of the table like a man born to it.

Michael's father Patrick raised his beer. "Thanks for putting this on," he said. "And congrats on selling the business, Leo. That's huge."

Leo Jr puffed up a little more. "Long haul, but we got there. Now the headache is figuring out what to do with the extra cash." He laughed, like this was a charming problem rather than a brag.

"Lucky you," Patrick said lightly. "Pretty sure Mikey and Dani wouldn't mind a bit of that to help plan their future."

The line was meant as a joke. It drove into Michael's chest like a stray nail.

"Fingers crossed for more little ones," Leo Sr boomed from midway down the table.

"What do you reckon, Gina?"

His wife flicked a napkin at him. "Leo, don't embarrass them."

Conversation splintered. Cutlery clinked louder. Someone asked for more bread; someone else asked about interest rates. The air thickened with steam and unsaid things.

Michael smiled where required. He chewed. He complimented the roast. His focus drifting to the photos on the wall – Leo Jr's brood on beaches and at theme parks, kids in matching outfits, all teeth and birthday candles.

Later, when bellies were full and chairs were placed back,

people spilled onto the front porch. Cigarettes flared; kids ran shrieking up and down the footpath, high on lemonade and cake.

"Beautiful lunch," Patrick said to Gina at the door. "We'll return the favour when we can."

"Our pleasure." Her eyes were soft. "Family's what matters."

Michael and Daniela made it as far as the Barina, waving behind them, before Leo Jr called from the top of the steps, glass aloft.

"Hey, Mikey, get home and get busy. Tick-tock, tick-tock."

The words chased them down the driveway.

In the driver's seat, Daniela's fingers tightened on the wheel.

"Your brother is something else," Michael muttered, fastening his seatbelt. "I know he means well, but that crap is getting old."

"I know," she said. "I'll talk to Mum, she'll tell him to shut up."

"I hope so," he replied. "Because if I do it, it won't land well."

She nodded, eyes on the road, thoughts focused elsewhere.

CHAPTER 7

BITTER DISAPPOINTMENT

Brisbane, late 1992 and mid-1992

The tension in the TAB continued to build like a taut spring as the pale woman in the corner started to sway. Michael intuitively tracked the movement with the shotgun.

"Don't … please don't point that thing at her," Hazel said quietly.

Michael eased the muzzle a fraction. The barrel still in the general vicinity, but not squarely at her.

"Everyone, stay still," he said. His breath came out muffled under the wool. "Nobody needs to get hurt."

A pedestal fan in the corner worked overtime. Half flapping in its breeze were withered green streamers. They had the same tired sag as the pastel balloons in the IVF clinic waiting room. Left up long after the open day he and Daniela had attended in happier times. His mind wandered back to a similar place, where hope was also heavily sold, but mostly underdelivered upon.

Brisbane, mid-1992. The fertility clinic smelled of disinfectant and other people's dreams going stale.

Daniela walked half a step ahead of him, manila folder clutched to her chest like a shield. They passed rows of plastic chairs crowded with couples. A woman in a power suit tapped at her briefcase with one foot, wedding ring flashing; a man in work boots sat hunched over his calloused hands. Everyone had the same look – tired, half-smiling, half-preparing for devastation.

As they sat, he noticed all the magazines scattered on a child-sized table. Smiling babies and happy nuclear families on every cover. Just what you wanted before someone told you what your body couldn't do.

"Mr and Mrs Whelan?" a nurse called, polite and neutral, like they were there about a parking fine.

They followed her into a consulting room. They sat. The aircon hummed. Somewhere out in the corridor, a phone rang on and on before someone bothered to pick it up.

He found himself reading the names on the cards because it was something to do with his eyes.

Our daughter, finally.

Our dream come true after so many years.

You gave us hope when we'd run out.

The door opened.

Dr Annabelle Jonze entered. Hair scraped back, no-nonsense glasses, the kind of expression you'd want on someone holding your future in an envelope. She smiled in a businesslike manner.

"Michael, Daniela – good to see you again. Sorry to keep you waiting," she said, settling in. "I've got your latest test results."

His insides clenched, sharp and sudden. Every time she opened a folder it felt like waiting for marks for an exam he hadn't studied for.

"There's no easy way to say this," she went on, looking between them. "Some of what I have to tell you today will be difficult."

Daniela's hand slid onto his knees and tightened. He stared at the doctor's mouth, trying to get ahead of the words by reading the shapes.

"The tests show that you have what we call Sertoli cell–only syndrome, Michael," she said. "Sometimes also referred to as Del Castillo syndrome."

The name hit like a blast of dry ice in the face. Clean, sharp, unhelpful.

"And what does that mean?" The edge in his voice, surprising, even to him.

"Mikey," Daniela said softly. "Let her explain. Please."

Dr Jonze nodded and clasped her fingers together.

"In simple terms," she said, "your testicles do not produce sperm. Your samples show nothing."

"So you're saying what?" he snapped. "That I'm faulty?"

Faulty wasn't the word he wanted, but it barged out first.

"So will I ever be able to produce children?"

The doctor measured herself.

"With this condition, conceiving naturally will be extremely unlikely," she replied.

"What about Daniela?" he asked, grasping at something he could fix. "You said her tests looked fine last time."

"They're still within normal ranges," Dr Jonze said. "There are no red flags on her side. This result is mostly about your biology, I'm afraid."

Daniela's fingers dug into his knee. He didn't look at her. If he did, everything in his chest might spill out on the sterile lino floor.

"What do we do now?" she asked, voice small.

"Are you telling me it's over?" he demanded. "No more IVF? No chance?"

"We're not saying 'no chance'," she replied. "But we are saying that the chance is minimal using standard approaches in Australia. There is some emerging work overseas in microdissection testicular surgery."

Daniela sat up a little straighter. "Where are they doing that?"

"There are a couple of centres in the United States," Dr Jonze said. "One in San Diego that's been publishing promising results. We don't have that level of microsurgical expertise here yet."

"So you're saying we have to fly to America," Michael cut in. "To the other side of the world, for some experimental fishing expedition."

"I'm saying that if you're determined to pursue a biological child using your sperm, that's the one avenue that might still offer a small chance," she said. "It's not a guarantee. Success rates vary. And it's expensive."

"How expensive?" Daniela asked, voice thin but controlled.

"By the time you add the surgery, the IVF cycles, medications, travel and accommodation," she said, "you could easily be looking at tens of thousands of dollars. Possibly more, depending on how many attempts you pursue."

A figure formed in Michael's head uninvited. Around fifty to seventy-five grand. More than they'd ever saved.

"I'll send you home with information on the surgical option and on donor programs. You don't need to rush anything. Let this news settle. You've had a long journey already."

She pushed a bundle of photocopied sheets across the desk. Diagrams. Bullet points. Smiling stock photo families.

Michael stared at the stack. It looked offensive.

They stepped out of Dr Jonze's office into a bright winter afternoon that seemed offensively ordinary.

Only the hiss of buses and the clunk of the car park boom gate. Other people walked past holding takeaway coffees and parking tickets, private worlds intact.

Daniela wrapped her arms around herself as they crossed the lot. The car keys shook in her hand when she unlocked the Barina.

Once they were inside with the doors shut, the outside noise muffled. He could hear her breathing.

"So," she said. One word, small and broken.

He stared through the windscreen at the ticket machine. "So I'm the problem," he said.

"Don't," she said. "Don't start that."

"It's true," he went on, words tumbling out too fast. "A diagnosis with a fancy name and basically zero sperm. My balls. My fault."

"This isn't about fault," she said. "They're cells that didn't form properly. It's biology, not a performance report card."

"Tell that to your brother," he muttered. "Tell that to your father. They sit at Sunday lunch surrounded by grandkids and I'm the freak at the table who can't get his act together."

Her teeth clenched. "Don't drag them into this," she said.

"So what then?" he said. "We sign up for this expensive surgery and travel halfway around the world? Cross our fingers some new age microscope finds one stray sperm hiding in there?"

"We need to look at it properly," she said. "Not just the brochure. Do further research. Understand the real odds. I don't want to be eighty, wondering if we should've tried."

"Or," he shot back, "we accept I'm broken and use some donor. And every time I look at our kid, I see the other bloke's face."

"That's not fair," she whispered. "Kids are more than DNA, Mikey. Your mum and dad made you the man I married through hard work, patience and love."

He looked away. His throat burned.

Daniela wiped at her eyes with the heel of her hand. Mascara smudged in thin grey arcs.

"We need to give ourselves time," she said. "We let the shock settle. Then we sit down, together, and work out what comes next. Like we promised we would."

He nodded, but the word 'together' scraped on something raw.

Together implied equal footing. He didn't feel equal; he felt useless, like he was her inferior.

On the drive home, he watched families at bus stops, kids climbing all over tired parents, teenagers rolling their eyes at each other. Every playground they passed felt like someone had painted *NOT FOR YOU* on the slide.

By the time they pulled into the driveway, something had set hard inside his chest. He wasn't going to be the man who shrugged and proclaimed, 'It is what it is'.

If there was a surgeon in San Diego who could scrape a single viable cell out of his useless biology, he was going to reach them. No matter what it cost.

CHAPTER 8

WHEN GOOD PEOPLE BREAK

Brisbane, late 1992 and mid-late 1992

Michael had been wielding the shotgun in the TAB for almost twelve minutes now, and his arms felt like concrete had been poured inside them.

Hazel stood rigid behind the counter, hands empty, till drawer wide open.

With the duffle bag full and waiting, it was time to make his escape.

He felt a new type of pressure build. The pressure of getting every step right if he wanted to walk back out of there cleanly and unidentified. It was a different feeling from the desperate, wild shove that had pushed him to the front door in the first place.

Three nights after the devastating meeting with Dr Jonze, Michael sat alone on the sofa.

He stared at the blank space between photos on the wall: holiday memories, birthdays and other celebrations coming to an abrupt halt. Just a square of paint.

Daniela had insisted on leaving it empty.

"We're saving it," she'd said, months earlier. "For our children's photos. First day of school, Christmas, all that."

"What are you thinking about, love?" Daniela asked as she lowered herself onto his lap. He usually relaxed when she did that. Tonight, it agitated him.

"Do you want to know?" he said.

"I suspect it's either about punching Leo Jr in the nose or about this wall with no photos of our little one," she said, mouth tilting wryly. "I'm not sure which."

"Half right," he sighed. "I'd love to smash your ignorant brother in the face, but he's not my priority at the moment."

"You know he isn't as bad as you think," she said. "He'd probably help with money for … all this, if we asked properly."

Michael gave a humourless snort. "No way. I am not turning up at Casa Bianchi, asking that bloke for charity. I couldn't stand him knowing every time we went to the clinic on his dollar."

"Okay then," she said. "Have you considered the other options Dr Jonze mentioned?"

His shoulders went rigid. "What options?"

"Donor sperm. Adoption. Different ways to make a family," she said, carefully. "We'd still be parents. It would take the pressure off you. Off us."

"What do you mean by *we*, Dani?" he asked. "You're not the one the doctor just told will probably never see their own eyes in their kid's face. You're not the one carrying around this … label."

"Michael," she said quietly, slipping off his lap, arms folding across her chest. "I know you're hurting. So am I. It's painful watching you beat yourself up over something you have no control over."

"No real reason to beat myself up?" His voice jumped. "That's easy for you to say."

She flinched.

"I didn't mean it like that," she said quickly. "I'm sorry. I just want you to know I'm here. I chose you. Not your sperm count."

He kept his eyes on the empty wall.

"You won't want me if I can't fix this," he said. The words came low and flat. "You married a man you believed would give you a whole family. If I'm not that man, then I'm not the man for you."

Silence settled, heavy and close.

"That's not true," she said, but it sounded like she was saying it from the other side of the suburb. "I didn't marry you for your ability to get me pregnant. I married you because you're kind, reliable, and you make me laugh."

He didn't answer. The effort of holding himself together took all his energy. If he looked at her face, at whatever hurt he'd put there, he wasn't sure what might come out of his mouth next.

She stood there a moment longer, then turned and walked down the hallway. The bedroom door clicked shut. The line of light underneath shrank and went out.

He stayed on the couch.

The following evening Michael sat on the living room floor, glass in hand, staring at his own ghosted face in the TV screen.

The whiskey bottle on the table was half peeled of its label.

Irish, bought on a special occasion. A taste of home that just tasted like resentment now.

He drained what was left in the glass. It didn't blunt anything. It just carved his anger into sharper edges.

Clinic diagrams floated up. Percentages and failure rates that boiled down to '*you're not manly enough to do what men are meant to do*'.

"How do I get us there?" His mind teleported to San Diego.

He picked up the scrap of paper where he'd scribbled costs earlier. Flights, accommodation, consult fees, procedure, follow-up. The numbers sat there like a bad joke.

They might as well have been coordinates to the moon.

"What if it worked?" he whispered. "What if just once, something went our way?"

The TV flickered on the nightly news. A wide shot of a suburban strip of shops filled the screen, yellow tape fluttering in the wind.

He leaned forward to turn up the volume.

"… no one was injured in the incident, but staff were left shaken after an armed robbery at this corner store in Stones Corner," the reporter stated.

Michael's curiosity rose.

The shop looked ordinary. The kind of place you ducked into for a bottle of milk or ciggies.

They cut to grainy security footage: a man in a balaclava, shoulders hunched, a long shape in his hands. The text at the bottom of the screen read: *Police seek information on armed robbery suspect.*

"Armed," Michael muttered. "Wonder if it was even real?"

The reporter continued. "Police describe the offender as approximately thirty, medium build, around 188 cm. Witnesses reported him running along Logan Road in an agitated state."

Michael let out a short snort. "No kidding."

The segment rolled on to petrol prices. He turned his head towards the couch.

"Could I do that?" he asked quietly. "Could I walk in, ask for the money, and walk out?"

His stomach flipped at the thought. The sensible part of his brain almost laughed. He was the bloke who turned up early, who gave cashiers back the dollar coin when they handed him too much change. Who said 'sorry' when other people bumped into him at pubs.

Not some delusional criminal.

He lined up the story of his life the way he lined up beams on a plan – all neat, straight lines. Study. Work hard. Pay tax. Help mates move house.

Put a bit away when there was any bit to put. Believe in the idea that if you did things right, life might meet you halfway.

The blank wall space. The empty spare room. The jokes at his expense.

His mind flicked back to that site meeting a few weeks earlier. Stuck at the lights on Gympie Road. Staring out the windscreen.

A TAB almost hidden in the strip of shops. Not one of the big, modernised city ones. An old little box with faded signage and ample car parking.

His thoughts intensified. Cash in the till. One entrance. Straight run back onto the main road. Cameras, sure, but nowhere near the sophistication of a bank. No security guard. No lunch-time queues.

His stomach clenched.

"It's not stealing," he heard himself say.

"It's a big Queensland-wide operation. Insurance will cover it. I take what we need, and they get it back eventually anyway. No one ends up worse off."

The story sounded like spin even as he manifested it.

I'm not a bad bloke.

I don't want to hurt anyone.

This is a one-off.

This is for us; for her.

In his head he was in the TAB already. Balaclava on. Something that looked like a gun in his hands. Quick in, quick out. No one hurt. A clean exit. A victimless crime.

He pictured the staff. Someone like Daniela behind that counter, maybe. Someone who'd then have to go home, lock the door twice, and jump every time a car backfired for months.

He didn't want to put that on a stranger.

He didn't want to look at himself and see a thug.

"This is madness," he said into the empty room. "Robbery? That's not me." Silence answered back.

He scraped a hand down his face and stood. Joints clicked in small protests. At the end of the hallway, the bedroom door was closed. He rested his forehead against the frame.

"I'll fix it," he whispered. "I swear to God, Dani. I'll fix it."

CHAPTER 9

THE WOMAN WHO FAINTS

Brisbane, late 1992

Claire Sutherland was not the fainting type, and especially not in a suburban TAB.

She had been the one who stayed upright when other people wilted. Patients, parents, colleagues collapsing in corridors – she was always the doctor they called when things started to go sideways.

Keeping her feet and keeping her head had been part of the job. Right up until the day the medical board slid a folder across a table and told her she was too great a risk to be allowed near a drug dispensary.

"Don't close your eyes," she told herself. "That's how you'll end up horizontal."

She shouldn't have been out in this heat. The walk from the bus stop on Gympie Road had felt endless, the unforgiving sun pressing down on her neck.

The TAB was the first shop to offer air-conditioning and a chair. She wasn't there to gamble. She'd come in to stop herself from keeling over on the footpath.

Her skin prickled. A wave of nausea washed up under her ribs. 'Oh, for fuck's sake', she thought. 'Not now'.

She swallowed hard, tried to breathe the way she told others to. In through the nose, out through the mouth, slow. Her chest refused to cooperate. The air felt thick, as if she were sucking it through gauze.

She reflected on a similar time when her breath had become shallow.

A community hall floated up in her mind. Blue plastic chairs, hot water urns, the moody hum of fluorescent lights. The smell of instant coffee and fear. A circle of people holding on to polystyrene cups and hope in equal measure.

"Hi, my name is Claire," she'd said, throat dry. "And I'm an alcoholic."

The room had welcomed her back. No drama. No judgement. Only kind recognition.

She hadn't fainted that night either. She'd wanted to. Had wanted the wooden floor to come up and swallow her whole when she'd stood in front of strangers and said the word she'd been dodging for years. Instead, she'd made herself stay upright, hands placed on the back of a chair until the wave passed.

If she could get through that, she told herself now, she could get through this. Shotgun and all.

Her body disagreed.

CHAPTER 10

THE DROP

Brisbane, late 1992

It had been around fifteen minutes since the man with the shotgun had terrorised Hazel and her customers, when she heard the thud.

A body hitting the floor had a particular sound.

Here, in the TAB, it was a dull knock against the tired carpeted floor and then nothing.

She didn't turn her head. Years behind the counter had trained her not to look away from the person with the complaint – or the weapon.

"Stay with me, lady," Hazel heard what she believed to be the scruffy man's voice—a slight twinge of a Scottish accent coming from near the trifecta board. "Just breathe. In, out. That's it."

Hazel kept her focus on the one who could still do the most damage: the idiot with the shotgun.

Hazel noted him shaking now. The gun had dropped lower. It was drooping, like the way a kid's arm sagged under the weight of a heavy school bag on the walk home.

Adrenaline couldn't sustain the journey, and gravity was taking over the battle.

"Keep your eyes on me, mate," Hazel said with the controlled measure usually reserved for a seasoned siege negotiator.

He reacted.

"Shut up, just … shut up. I'm in fucking control here."

He swung the barrel wider, taking them all in. Hazel's heart kicked hard enough to make her vision stutter.

He started walking backwards.

Hazel noticed the shotgun was wet with sweat; she also saw his looming challenge coming well before he did.

As he continued to move backwards at a faster pace, he walked straight onto a single plastic chair precariously placed behind him. It folded underneath him.

He tried to hold his balance but couldn't. He collapsed awkwardly.

In an attempt to break his fall, he manoeuvred both hands so that the palms were parallel to the carpeted floor.

One gesture of self-preservation led to the surrender of another.

The shotgun lay on the ground. The robber tried to grasp at it, but it was now outside his reach, and he was tangled up.

Hazel moved before fear had a chance to vote.

She lunged across the gap. Years of grabbing cups, of catching falling glasses and toppling form guides, had built a certain kind of reflex. This was heavier, more dangerous, but the basic principle was the same: get there first.

Her fingers closed around the stock, almost as fast as it had slipped from his.

Hazel pulled it in against her chest, stock thumping her collarbone, the sheer weight of it shocking a grunt out of her.

"Jesus," the Hilfiger man muttered.

Hazel brought the gun up; the barrel wasn't pointed perfectly, but it was now aimed at the right person and not her innocent customers.

Hazel risked a glance toward the scruffy man with the Scottish accent.

He had already started to tend to the lady who had fainted. A pile of newspapers provided a pillow for her weary head to rest.

"You're okay," he murmured to the woman on the floor. "You had a bit of a turn, that's all. I've got you. Stay with me."

"TAB lady," Hilfiger man yelled from the back of the room. "Where is your phone? I will call the police."

"Not just yet, handsome," she clapped back. Surprised by her own swagger.

All her training and experience taught her to get the police involved immediately in the event of an armed robbery. You let the uniforms deal with it. You hand over the statements, then go home and cry yourself to sleep.

Her finger tightened on the stock.

"TAB lady," the bearded Scotsman enquired. "You alright up there?"

"Just fine," she said.

She dropped her chin at the man on the floor.

"Stop looking like you're about to bolt. You won't get far with me watching you. And take that woollen beanie off your face."

He removed the balaclava defeatedly and lifted his head.

Hazel inspected his facial features. Up close, beyond the mask, he didn't look like a monster. He looked like every other bloke she'd seen hunched over a form guide, turning loss into habit.

"I didn't want to hurt anyone," he said hoarsely. "I just … needed the money."

Hazel pushed it aside bluntly. Empathy could wait.

"Save it for the minute," Hazel barked at him. "I need time to think."

Her mind wandered to her own need for money. Her last twenty thousand in cash under the counter, and Craig. She had told herself, over and over, that he couldn't possibly know about the twenty thousand she had hived off for her own benefit.

But now, staring at the idiot on the floor and the strangers scattered through her TAB, she wasn't so sure. Had Craig sent this bloke? Was Hilfiger in on it? The Scot? Even the pale woman on the carpet? What if they were all just pieces on Craig's chessboard?

"Right, before we do anything else, I need to know who the hell you lot are, and what the heck you're doing in my shop today."

CHAPTER 11

THE CREW IN THE ZOO

Brisbane, late 1992

"Okay, let's start with you, the idiot who decided to walk in here and terrorise us all," Hazel said with conviction, shifting the barrel a fraction, not quite pointing at the robber's head, but close enough.

He swallowed. Without the mask, he looked younger than she'd expected.

"My name's Michael," he said. "Michael Whelan."

The name seemed to hang in the air. Hazel watched the others register it.

"Alright, Michael Whelan," Hazel said. "And why are you in my shop, waving a shotgun around?"

He glanced at the duffle bag, at the open till drawer.

"I needed the money," he said. "I never came here to hurt anybody."

Hazel raised an eyebrow.

"Everyone needs more money, matey. That's why this place exists, but most don't need a weapon to achieve that desire. So, you'd want to start talking some sense real fast."

He hesitated, then something inside him gave way. Whatever thin bravado the balaclava had given him was gone.

"My wife and I … we've been trying to have a baby," he said, words stumbling at first, then gathering pace. Years now. They finally told us it's me. My DNA. Some fancy syndrome. I don't have any sperm that works."

Hazel felt the odd sensation that the wider world was listening, even the TV commentary seemed quieter under the weight of his confession.

"There is a clinic in San Diego," Michael went on. "It would be our only chance of having a biological child, but it costs a fortune, and we'd already burned through our savings on IVF rounds that didn't work."

He let out a shaky breath.

"So, I decided to walk in here, wave a gun, and try to take home the money from the till to help fund our trip to America."

"Right," Hazel said, forcing herself not to soften. "So that's Michael. Wants to be a dad and picked the worst possible way to try to fund it. Possibly a jam stripe short of an Iced Vo Vo biscuit, as my late husband Jim liked to say."

She shifted her glare to Hilfiger Shirt.

"You. What's your name, and what are you doing here? You don't dress like my typical clientele, nor do you look like the type that needs more money like the baby bandit here."

The well-groomed man's jaw tightened at that comment, pride pricked. He straightened his belt out of habit, as if appearances still mattered.

"Charlie Hinton," he said. "I'm … in law. Corporate, mostly."

"Of course you are," Hazel said dryly. "And let me guess, you live in an eight-bedroom house on acreage in Bridgeman Downs?"

Charlie let out a humourless laugh.

"Sad but true, lady," he confessed.

"I came here today to escape," he said. "Put a few bets on. Watch the numbers run. Ten minutes where I'm not the person everyone expects to fix things." "My father runs a share trading business," he went on. "You may have read about him in the Courier Mail? He is under investigation by ASIC for insider trading. And I work for ASIC."

"I know he's guilty," he said. "He knows I know he's guilty. But he is pressuring me to be a good son, to protect the family name," Charlie said in a defeated tone.

"Plus, my wife cares more about the fancy lifestyle she may lose if my father has the book thrown at him, as opposed to me upholding the law."

Charlie briefly observed the TV, where horses circled at some distant track.

"At least here I can get lost in numbers on a screen and forget about my so-called fantastic life others judge me for."

He gave Michael a quick, sideways look.

"I've got twin girls," he added, voice dropping. "Five altogether. They still think I'm a hero. They're the only thing stopping me from putting a bullet in my own story some days."

Hazel felt the energy in the TAB shift into even darker territory, if possible, and she didn't know what to say or where to look next.

"I'm sorry to hear all that, Charlie." That was all she could muster.

She swung the barrel a fraction towards the back of the room.

"You're next, Scotsman."

The scruffy bloke with the scarred knuckles grinned at the nickname.

"Name's Angus," he said. "Angus Stenhouse."

His accent wrapped around the syllables, Glasgow clinging stubbornly to Brisbane air.

"And why are you in my shop today, Angus Stenhouse?" Hazel asked. "Besides catching falling women?"

He shrugged, broad shoulders rolling under the threadbare singlet.

"Habit, mostly," he said. "Places like this feel familiar. Noise, odds, blokes kidding themselves they've cracked the code. But today, I'm here for something specific."

Hazel's grip tightened.

"Here to make some real money before I'm sent back to the tin pail."

"Tin pail?" Hazel asked.

"Jail, pretty much my second home of recent years."

Angus glared at Michael.

"And before you start judging," he added, "At least my stupidity doesn't involve pointing weapons at defenceless ladies."

Michael nodded in agreement.

"Oh yeah, and no kiddies for me," Angus said, almost as an afterthought. "I'm not fit for it. Don't think I'm shooting blanks, however." He looked at Michael again with a wry smile.

"Now tell me, Angus aka Billy Connolly," Hazel interjected. "Does your 'something specific' for today have anything to do with an accountant named Craig?"

"Who?" Angus enquired, confused. "I don't know any fookin Craig lady, it's a great name for someone with a boring, shite job like an accountant, however."

Hazel couldn't help but let out a slight chuckle and trust what he was saying to constitute the truth.

"Just to put your mind at rest, lady, a race is set to be run today, and the winner is already decided. My job is to make sure the right people profit from this information."

Hazel blew out a breath.

"Right," she said. "We also have Angus with a dodgy race."

Her focus shifted to the woman now sitting in the plastic chair. The colour was back in her cheeks now. She sat upright, one hand braced on the plastic arm, eyes clearer than they had any right to be after being horizontal on a grubby TAB floor.

"And you, love?" Hazel asked, softening her tone. "What's your name, besides 'the woman who gave us all a fright'?"

The woman wet her lips, checked with her fingers that her head was not bleeding.

"Claire," she said. "Claire Sutherland."

"Alright, Claire Sutherland," Hazel said. "Why are you in Aspley, in my TAB, in this heat, collapsing on my carpet?"

Claire let out a small, disbelieving laugh.

"I shouldn't be," she said. "I was trying to get to Chermside. There's a group meeting I'm meant to attend there. I got off at the wrong bus stop, the sun hit me like a hammer, and I felt like I was going to throw up or black out on the footpath."

She glanced at the doorway, as if remembering the stumble in.

"I saw the sign for the TAB and thought, air-conditioning. Chairs. Somewhere to sit until my legs remembered what they're for."

She drew a breath, slower this time.

"I'm a doctor," she said. "Well. I was. Paediatrics. Before the medical board suspended me." Her mouth twisted around the words. "I've been drinking too long and too hard. Finally caught up with me. I'm on new meds, cutting back. My body's having a tantrum about it."

She gave Hazel a tired, embarrassed look.

"I'm usually the one standing in a resus bay telling people to breathe," she said. "Today I'm the idiot who nearly fainted in a betting shop."

"No idiots here," Hazel said. "Just people whose lives have gone sideways at the same time."

Charlie shifted his weight, as if acknowledging that sideways was generous. Angus nodded once, slowly. Michael stared at the floor, as if trying to find a version of himself that hadn't ended up here.

Hazel realised they were all looking back at her now.

"And you?" Charlie asked quietly. "You know all of us now, or enough of us. Who are you, besides the TAB lady holding the shotgun?"

She almost said, 'Nobody. Just a widow in a faded green polo'. Instead, she lifted her head.

"I'm Hazel Andrews," she said. "This is my shop."

"My late husband bought into this place on a big promise." When he died, the debts stayed. The clever man with the certificates on his wall, Craig, whom I mentioned before, suggested I sell before the bank took the lot. I decided I wasn't ready to hand my keys to a man who helped put me into this predicament to start with."

She hitched the gun a little higher.

"So instead of doing the sensible thing, I've been trying to keep the lights on. Hiding what I can. Making one last stupid play before they drag me out by the ankles."

Hazel managed a small smile.

"Congratulations," she said. "You've all picked a terrible day to wander into Hazel Andrews' late-life catastrophe."

For a moment, absurdly, there was the ghost of a chuckle in the room. It died quickly, but it was there.

Michael rubbed his face with both hands.

"So, what now?" he asked. "You've got our names and our sob stories. Do you get Angus and Charlie to lock me in the broom cupboard until the police arrive?"

Hazel considered him.

"You're not going anywhere," she said. "Not yet. Passing this whole mess onto the police puts it in the hands of people who don't care about the why. They'll see an armed robbery, a woman who ended up out cold, a bent horse race if Angus is telling the truth, and a shop owner with not much left to her name who also mysteriously has twenty thousand dollars in cash under the counter."

Charlie looked at Hazel in shock.

"What do you mean by twenty thousand in …"

"Fook me," Angus cut Charlie off and ran towards the totaliser screen.

CHAPTER 12

THE SACRED PACT

Brisbane, late 1992

O n the TV above the counter, the guide flicked over:
ALICE SPRINGS – RACE 7 – COMING UP

Angus leaned forward, squinting at the screen.

"That's it," he said. "Alice Springs. Race 7."

Hazel shifted the shotgun on her aching shoulder.

"What?" she asked.

"The race," Angus replied. "The something specific. The one Mac told me about."

"Mac?" Charlie asked.

"Macready," Angus said. "Colin Macready. We did time together at Wacol."

Hazel had learned the hard way not to ask too many questions about favours from jail, but the day had bulldozed past that line.

"This had better be more than punter's gossip," she said. "I've heard enough about 'sure things' that fell in a heap lately."

Angus's mouth twisted.

"It's not gossip," he said. "Macready runs debt collection,

enforcement, and … discouragement. Sometimes he makes sure certain horses run in ways that suit certain bank accounts."

Charlie stared. "So the race is fixed?"

"I'm saying it's been arranged," Angus replied. "Quietly."

"And this Macready, can he be trusted?" Claire asked. "Because he sounds like the opposite."

"He's dangerous," Angus said, "but he's kept his word with me. If he says something happens, it usually does."

Hazel forced herself to keep her tone even.

"What's the name of the horse, if it's going to win, I want to know."

Angus watched the runners scroll past.

"Trimax," he said. "Number four. Drops out the back, looks beaten, then runs over the top of them. That's the arranged plan."

"Trimax sounds more like weed killer than a racehorse," Charlie muttered.

"Names don't win races," Angus said. "Arrangements do."

Claire shifted against the leg of the plastic chair, colour creeping back into her face.

"Have I missed a meeting?" she asked. "Because last thing I remember, someone was waving a shotgun around and we were all terrified. Now you're talking like we're a syndicate."

Angus met her gaze. "You got a better idea, doc?"

"Yes," Claire said. "Call the police. Hand in the gun. Go home. Live long enough to complain about it in therapy."

"Claire, please excuse my language lovely," Hazel said, "but this TAB, men, and the racing industry have been fucking me over for too long. Maybe this is my one chance to finally fuck them back."

Charlie let out a low whistle. "Alright," he said. "That's one opinion on the table."

Angus nodded at the duffle bag full of the shop's takings on the counter.

"Here's the reality," he said. "If the cops turn up, they seize it. The TAB head office, insurers, probably the ATO come sniffing. They don't just look at the bag. They look at everything."

Hazel felt her stomach turn. She'd been keeping one thought locked up in a mental drawer labelled 'later'. Angus had just prised it open.

"And that's where my twenty comes in," she said quietly.

"Your what?" Claire asked.

Charlie's head snapped round. "Twenty?"

Hazel could feel the three of them watching her.

"I've got twenty thousand in cash here also," she said. "It's under the counter in a nylon bag. I kept it off the books and took it out of the bank so that vulture accountant couldn't grab it."

"Holy shit Hazel." Angus exclaimed.

"I'd love to think the coppers would never find it, but the second they walk in here they will also sniff out the mystery cash. That twenty and this duffle bag with takings might as well be holding hands."

"If the police do this by the numbers," Charlie said, slipping into his careful, analytical voice, "all the money becomes evidence. The robbery bag. The twenty thousand. Anything extra they find. Months, maybe years, before any of it is released. And in the meantime, every ledger tied to this place gets turned over."

"And Craig gets dragged into it," Hazel finished, "whether I like it or not. He'd love that."

On the TV: RACE 7 – FIVE MINUTES.

Hazel drew a breath that hurt.

"Alright Charlie" she said. "Lay out the options for us here."

Charlie adjusted his tailored shorts, the nervous energy evident.

"Option A. We call the police. Hazel gets stripped bare through audits, Michael goes in cuffs, Angus misses the chance to maximise the fixed race opportunity, and the rest of us hope the story sounds noble when we tell it in ten years' time."

"Which is still technically the correct option," Claire muttered.

"Maybe on paper," Hazel said. "But not for me. I'm sick of paper."

"Option B," Charlie continued. "We accept we're already deep in it. We use what Angus knows. We decide for ourselves what happens to the money and what happens to us."

"And we just let a criminal walk free," Claire stated.

The corner of Michael's mouth twitched, but he said nothing.

"Michael's not a criminal," Hazel snapped.

The words surprised her.

"Not in the bone-deep way," she added. "He's a desperate idiot trying to pay for something the universe won't give him. That's different to someone who makes a living hurting people."

"And what does that make me?" Angus asked, almost lightly.

"You're the man who hasn't let her out of your sight yet," Hazel said, nodding at Claire. "And the one who knows enough about criminal activity to both scare me and be useful at the same time."

She blew out a breath. "Charlie. Least-worst option. Hurry. Go."

He pinched the bridge of his nose.

"If we quietly put the duffle money back in the till," he said, "on paper this TAB finishes the day like any other. No big unexplained loss, no sudden windfall. That's the only version where head office doesn't immediately start asking questions."

Hazel nodded. "The contents in the duffle go back in the till. That's easy."

"But what about my twenty under the counter?" she asked. "If anyone official finds out I've had it here, I'm done anyway. At least if I stake it, it's a risk I chose."

She straightened her shoulders.

"Here's what I'm putting on the table," she said. "We put the duffle back. We treat my twenty as the stake. And before Angus makes a single call, we make a pact. Properly. No half-hearted nonsense."

Charlie's gaze went to the duffle bag, then back to her.

"Putting the duffle back is rational," he said. "Putting your twenty on a race Macready's touched is still mad, but it's calculated mad. Just don't ask me to pretend this isn't laundering and concealment."

"I'm not asking you to pretend," Hazel said. "I'm asking if you're in."

On the TV: RACE 7 – FOUR MINUTES.

Claire gave a short, incredulous laugh.

"You want to make a sacred pact over a dirty bet," she said.

"No," Hazel replied. "I want the pact over us."

Angus's eyes narrowed, sharpening.

"I need to see it," he said.

Hazel frowned. "You don't trust me?"

"It's not that," he said. "If I tell Macready there's twenty on the table and it's thin air, he'll take it personal. I'm done taking things personal from him."

Hazel jerked her chin.

"Fine. Come round. Mind my knees."

He slipped through the swing gate. Hazel bent, grunting with effort, and dragged the nylon bag onto the counter. She unzipped it. The neat bricks of cash sat there, quiet and accusing.

"There," she said. "Twenty thousand reasons I should've told Jim and Craig where to shove their plans."

Angus counted by sight, quick and practised, then zipped it closed again and pushed it back towards her.

"It's real," he said. "One bad run and it's gone."

Hazel looked from the bag to Michael, Claire, Charlie.

"If I do nothing," she said, "Craig and the bank eat me alive anyway. At least this way I get to choose who has the first bite. Charlie, can you live with that?"

He hesitated, then nodded slowly.

"I can live with it," he said. "I won't pretend it's clean. But it's internally consistent."

Hazel blew out a breath.

"I'm tired of everyone else holding the chalk," she said. "So this is it. This race is our sacred seventh. One line we step over together. Not a doorway we keep going through."

Michael's voice came out rough.

"If there's any version of today where my wife still gets her chance," he said, "I want it."

Hazel nodded once.

"The pact is this," she said. "Listen carefully."

"We put my twenty on Trimax. We put the duffle money back in the till so the TAB looks normal. If Trimax loses, we still walk out of here and get on with our lives. No police. No confessions. We wear it. All of it. And we never speak of today again. Not to partners, friends, therapists, priests. This room keeps the story."

"If Trimax wins, first thing is Hazel Andrews gets her neck out of the noose. My debts, this TAB, anything that lets Craig and the bank stop owning me – that gets paid. Clean."

"After that, whatever's left is split evenly. One share each. Including Michael. No side deals. No skimming. What you do with your share is your business."

"And Angus," she added, "you take that gun and make sure it never sees daylight again. I don't care how."

Angus's mouth twitched. "I know a skip or two," he said.

At that, Michael cleared his throat.

"About the gun," he said. "Just … in the spirit of full disclosure."

Hazel became suddenly aware of its weight in her hands. She nudged the barrel a little closer to the floor.

"What about it?" she asked.

"It's not loaded," he said. "Can't be. It's a replica. Looks nasty, but it's never been able to fire. I couldn't bring myself to walk in here with the real thing."

Silence dropped over them.

"You're telling me this thing isn't even real?" Hazel asked.

"Metal and wood, yeah," Michael said. "Mechanically, no. I stripped it. There's no firing pin. I swear."

A hot, tangled mix of fury and relief fizzed in her chest.

"You stupid, stupid man," she said. "You could've shared that earlier."

Angus snorted. Claire let out a tiny, unbelieving huff.

"Well, that's one less thing to keep me up at night," Hazel said. "But it doesn't change what you did. It just means when you walk out of here, you're not walking away from four people you nearly killed. Only four people you scared half to death."

She turned back to the group.

"Right," she said. "You've heard the terms. Win or lose, no police. No talking. If the horse runs like Angus says, I clear my debts and the rest gets split evenly, including Michael. Angus gets rid of the useless gun. That's the pact."

She fixed Angus with a look.

"You in?"

He held her gaze, then nodded.

"I'm in," he said. "I've spent years doing favours for blokes like Macready. I won't lose sleep about taking a slice back."

"Charlie?" Hazel asked.

He glanced at the TV, then at Michael.

"I'm in," he said. "One race. One pact. No sequels. Ever."

"No sequels," Hazel agreed. "Claire?"

Claire stared at the ceiling one last time, then at Michael, then Hazel.

"I'm in," she said. "And I'm telling God about it silently every day until I die. But I'm in."

Hazel looked to Michael.

"Last one," she said. "Yes or no?"

"Yes," he said. "I already ruined who I was when I walked in here. I'd rather at least try to make something good out of it."

Hazel let out a breath that felt like it had been jammed in her ribs for months.

"Done," she said. "The pact stands. The money in the duffle goes back in the till. My twenty goes on Trimax. The fake shotgun and balaclava go under the counter and Angus disposes of them later."

"If the horse loses, we carry it. If it wins, we fix what we can and live with the rest. And we never speak of today again."

"Alright, Scotsman," she said. "The sacred seventh is set. Now you make the calls."

CHAPTER 13

THE CALLS

Brisbane, late 1992

Angus wiped his palms on his ruggers shorts and slipped in behind the counter. The little swing gate had never looked like much, but seeing a man his size slide through it rattled Hazel more than the shotgun had.

"Careful with the phone," she said. "Telecom took three weeks to fix it last time a customer roughly handled it."

"Wouldn't dream of upsetting Telecom," he said.

He lifted the receiver. He dialled the number from memory.

The line rang once, twice, then clicked.

"Yeah?" a voice said. Gruff. Flat.

"Macready," Angus said, his voice dropping half a shade. "It's me. Angus."

"Thought you'd gone quiet," Macready said. "You at the shop?"

"I am," Angus said. "Watching Alice Springs Race 7 scroll up."

"Good," Macready said. "You know the drill. How much you got on the nose of four?"

Angus glanced at Hazel's nylon bag.

"Twenty," he said. "Twenty grand. On Trimax."

A pause.

"That's more than we discussed," Macready said. "You find a money tree, Gus?"

"Situation changed," Angus said. "It's not all mine. There are people here who lose more than rent money if this goes sideways. I need to know how solid this is Mac?"

Another pause. When Macready spoke again, his tone had cooled.

"Trimax doesn't lose," he said. "Not today. Not this race. Not after the work that's gone in. If you're holding twenty, get it on. I don't care whose notes they are when the accounts get fed."

"That fixed enough for you?" Macready added. "Or do you want proof posted in pieces?"

"That's fine," he said. "And we're square after this right Mac."

"You're square when I say you're square," Macready said. "But this'll do. Place the bet. Don't get clever. Don't make me come looking."

The line went dead.

For a second, all Angus could hear was the hiss of the handset.

He hung up, then picked it back up again.

"Who are you calling now?" Claire asked.

"The SP Bookmakers," he said. "Macready pulls strings. Someone still has to write the ticket."

He dialled again.

"Alice Springs Chinese Takeaway," a sarcastic voice answered.

"It's Gus, you dickhead," Angus said.

"Use authorised account number 5. Trimax, Race 7, Alice Springs. Twenty thousand. On the nose."

There was a low whistle and the clatter of keys.

"Big punt," the man said.

"Righto. Trimax, Race 7, twenty thousand on the nose. You're set."

"Cheers," Angus said, and hung up.

He turned to the others.

"That's it," he said. "Bet's on. No going back now."

On the TV: RACE 7 – TWO MINUTES TO START.

"Right," she said. "We've made the pact and the bet's live. Now we do the boring bit."

"The what?" Michael asked.

"We try look ordinary," Hazel said. "Michael, you sit in that chair like any other punter who lost his shirt on the last race. Claire, you stay put. Angus, off the counter. Charlie, pretend you're actually reading those form guides."

They moved into position.

Michael sank into a plastic chair, clasping his hands to stop them shaking.

Charlie hovered near the racks, eyes flicking over numbers he wasn't seeing, flipping pages every so often.

Claire sat upright, arms folded, watching the TV as if it was a monitor in recovery.

Angus leaned against the wall, ankles crossed, expression neutral.

Hazel straightened pens that didn't need straightening and wiped a counter that was already clean. From the street, through the glass, it might have looked like any other slow afternoon in a tired Brisbane TAB.

On the TV, the caption jumped: RACE 7 – ONE MINUTE TO START.

A race caller's lips moved in silence. Trimax circled in the mounting yard, flank shining, ears flicking. A horse with no idea five strangers half a country away had just staked their futures on its hooves.

Outside, tyres crunched on gravel.

Hazel's eyes lifted, automatically tracking the movement past the window.

Blue and white slid into view – familiar livery, quiet and deliberate, like something predatory under shallow water.

The police sedan eased into a bay right outside the door.

Hazel's pulse spiked. Her grip tightened on the shotgun.

"That's Donnelly's car," she whispered. "Senior Sergeant Donnelly."

The engine cut out.

Hazel swallowed, never taking her eyes off the glass.

"Looks like Race 7 isn't the only gamble we're taking today," she said.

CHAPTER 14

DONNELLY'S BET

Brisbane, late 1992

Hazel watched, stomach clenching as Donnelly unfolded himself from the seat, stretched, and put on his Queensland Police cap.

"Mate of yours?" Angus asked quietly.

"Senior Sergeant Donnelly," Hazel said. "He pops in for a flutter and a gossip. Thinks he's God's gift to the local community."

"And is he?" Angus said.

"Hopefully not today," Hazel muttered nervously.

"Charlie, go pull that crowbar out of the door handles so he can get in and flick the sign back to OPEN."

"Angus, make sure that crowbar, fake shotgun, balaclava and duffle bag are well hidden under the counter, somewhere next to the nylon bag is fine."

"Everyone, try to look normal, no obvious panic signs."

Donnelly pushed open the door without hurry and stepped inside, bringing a waft of warm air and authority with him. He moved the way long-serving cops did, like the room belonged to him unless proven otherwise.

Hazel put on her TAB smile. It felt brittle, stretched over nerves. "Afternoon, Sergeant," she said. "Keeping us all out of trouble?"

"Doing my best, Haze." He tipped his hat. His eyes skimmed around the room, taking in Michael, Angus, Charlie, Claire in her chair, before coming back to Hazel. "Quiet one. You scared everyone off with your hot tips?"

"Recession's doing the heavy lifting there," she said. "What drags you away from all that exciting paperwork?"

"Feature race in the Alice." He leaned on the counter, casual as a man at a bar. "Thought I'd see if I can finally impress the missus, maybe shout her some new perfume with the winnings. She reckons my punting record is a crime in itself."

"Hahaha," Hazel forced a laugh.

On the TV behind him, adverts still ran; jingles, cheap Gold Coast holidays. Any second, the feed would switch back to red dirt and horses.

"Race 7?" she asked, the question out too fast.

He smiled. "Yeah, I'm a sucker for a feature. Favourite looks solid. What do you reckon, certainty? Or am I about to donate to the Queensland State Government again?"

Hazel's mouth felt dry.

"Red Dingo's honest," she said. "Turns up. Never does anything too dramatic."

Charlie watched Donnelly with the wary focus he usually reserved for white-collar frauds. Men like this could ruin you with a line in a report – and call it public service.

For a moment, he saw himself the way Donnelly might if any of this came to light: mid-level suit, wrong friends, a little too close to money that moved in odd ways. The idea made his neck prickle.

"You getting on, Sergeant?" Angus asked, tone easy. "Or just here to heckle the callers?"

"Five each way on Red Dingo, the fave," Donnelly said, tapping the form guide with two fingers.

"Living dangerously there, Sergeant." Angus chirped.

Hazel took Donnelly's cash. Her hands wanted to shake; she didn't let them. Muscle memory did the work while her brain was elsewhere.

If Trimax wins: twenty grand at seventy-to-one. Less whatever slice Angus's contact took. Plenty to put distance between her and the wolves, and everyone else to live with a little less stress for a while.

If Trimax didn't fire; she couldn't let herself go there.

The machine chirped. The ticket slid out. She tore it free and handed it across the counter.

"There you go," she said. "Red Dingo. Here's hoping it makes the bookies angry."

"Cheers." Donnelly tucked the ticket carefully into his shirt pocket, as it mattered more than the fivers he usually threw at midweek races.

"You putting your twenty cents' worth on anything Haze?"

"Not today, Sarge. Focused on keeping the lights on at the minute," Hazel said. "You staying to watch?"

She knew the answer before she heard it.

"Wouldn't miss it," he said. "Got half an hour before the boss starts asking questions."

Hazel gave a thin laugh. "Well, you know where the coffee is if you feel like testing the limits of human endurance. Milk's probably still alright."

"Reckon I'll live dangerously only once today," he said, his gaze now fixated on the TV.

Michael was trying to look like any other bloke who'd popped in on his lunch break; hands in pockets, weight on one leg, eyes glued to the wall-mounted form guides.

Charlie shifted a fraction so he could see the Sergeant, the doorway and the race on the screen without moving his head. If Donnelly so much as sniffed that something was off, Charlie wanted the earliest possible warning.

Angus remained calm. The call to Alice was done. The money sat in Trimax's name. And now a docile cop was lurking around; the threat level was more akin to a mosquito than a saltwater crocodile.

Claire sat in the chair, sipping from a bottle of water and looking genuinely disinterested in all that was happening around her.

On the screen, the camera swung to the desert course, Alice Springs' very own Dave Douglas's dulcet tones started to fill the airwaves.

"And they're headed to the starters gate here in Alice Springs, ladies and gentlemen. We're almost all set for the running of the feature race. The Piggly Supermarket's Outback Dash."

Hazel couldn't help pondering if their lives were on the precipice of a critical before-and-after moment, with Senior Sergeant Donnelly, standing right there to witness whichever way it fell.

CHAPTER 15

RACE 7

Brisbane, late 1992

They all found ways to look at the TV without looking at each other.

Hazel planted herself behind the counter, above where all the evidence was hidden.

Senior Sergeant Donnelly leaned on the side bench, playing with a pen that had broken from its safety rope. His betting slip peeked out above his shirt pocket, Red Dingo ticket tucked away like an insurance policy.

"Here we go," he said, not taking his focus off the screen. "C'mon, ya red beauty. Don't make a fool of me in front of Hazel again."

"I'm sure the horse lies awake worrying about your reputation, Sergeant," Hazel said.

Her voice sounded normal. It didn't feel it.

The track looked like a circle of green painted onto red dirt that stretched for as far as the eye could register. Sun glared off rails and helmets. Horses circled behind the gates, bright silks letting them jog and sidestep the last nerves out.

"Field of eight," Dave Douglas announced, voice rolling through the TAB's speakers. "Favourite here, Red Dingo, well tried. Bit of late interest for Trimax, odds have tightened here on track a little for the long shot after some late nibbles."

Hazel's shoulders twitched at the news. Late nibbles. She pictured anonymous hands all over the country sliding money in under other people's bets. Macready's web tightening.

"The racing industry fleecing poor honest citizens again. I wouldn't even back that Trimax nag with my mother-in-law's money." Donnelly proclaimed as his attempt at humour went unappreciated by the room.

"Red Dingo goes forward … Trimax walks up, ears pricked … and they're set …"

"Jumping … now."

Gates crashed back. Eight masses of muscle leapt forward.

"Red Dingo bounced out sweetly, sitting handy near the front with a line of bright colours across the course. Trimax flopped out the back, last by two lengths, looking half-asleep."

"Don't you dare be too clever," Hazel muttered under her breath.

The first furlong went past as the odds anticipated. The well-backed horses found the rail near the front or middle of the field. The second-rate horses were caught wide, over-racing and wasting fuel. And Trimax plodded along behind them, exactly where a mug punter would have given up on its chances.

Donnelly slapped his thigh, like he was riding the favourite home.

"Beautiful," he said. "Perfect sit. Just keep him slightly off the rail, little man."

Hazel barely heard him. Her pulse thudded in her ears. Twenty thousand dollars sat out there in a horse that looked like it wouldn't qualify for a two-year-old's barrier trial, let alone a feature race.

Beside the form guides, Charlie tried to calculate and failed. His brain had nothing to anchor onto. The numbers were irrelevant, the variables compromised by human intervention.

Claire breathed in, out, in, out. She told herself she was calming her nervous system and not simply trying not to puke from adrenaline.

At the six-hundred mark, Dave Douglas' tone sharpened.

"Red Dingo travelling nicely … the favourite poised to pounce … runners fanning wider now looking for their runs … and Trimax still last, hasn't peeled yet …"

"Any time you like, sweetheart," Angus growled at the TV.

As they hit the four-hundred-mark, something changed.

On screen, Trimax's jockey shifted the whip in his hands. The horse pricked its ears as if someone had whispered to it from above. The gap between him and the pack started to shrink.

"There," Angus said softly.

"Trimax now starting to pick up … still with a wall of horses in front of him, but he's beginning to thread through …"

Hazel's stomach dropped. It looked impossible, too many legs, too little room. She could feel Michael's presence near her, praying for hope but accustomed to the opposite.

Red Dingo kicked clear, the favourite's green and white pulling a length in front. Donnelly pulled the ticket out of his shirt pocket.

"Go on!" he yelled at the TV. "Kick, ya mongrel!"

"Two hundred left to run … Red Dingo in front … challengers coming … here's Trimax, flashing down the outside …"

On the camera angle it looked like a smear of dark bay and bright colours, hooves blurred, red dirt flying. Hazel's breath stuck. The whole TAB leaned towards the screen by instinct.

"One hundred to go … Red Dingo still … but Trimax is flying late.

"Red Dingo, Trimax … Trimax dives right on the line …photo!"

The camera froze on the post, horses lunging, nostrils flared, jockeys lunged forward.

Donnelly slapped his ticket against his palm, eyes narrowed.

"Hope they've got a good angle," he said. "Looked like my boy hung on there."

Hazel's legs tingled, pins and needles darting up from her feet.

"Come on," Angus whispered. "Come on, you beautiful, rigged bastard …"

The screen flipped to a still, zoomed in on the post. Two noses, one just in front.

PHOTO – 4 FROM 1

"And there it is punters, Trimax has stormed home late from the back of the field to defeat Red Dingo by the smallest of margins. The bookies are rejoicing here trackside in the Alice."

The official results appeared on the screen.

RESULT: 1ST – 4 TRIMAX

2ND – 1 RED DINGO

3RD – 6 DESERT SWING

Donnelly stared at the screen.

"You have got to be bloody kidding me," he said. "Thing was seventy-to-one."

Hazel swallowed.

"That's racing, Sergeant" was all she managed.

Donnelly blew out his cheeks, then laughed, shaking his head.

"I should know better than to back a red dog," he said. "Should've boxed that four in a trifecta, hey, Hazel? Imagine the payout."

She made a non-committal facial expression.

He turned back to face her properly for the first time since the race jumped.

"You alright, Haze? You've gone a bit pale around the gills," Donnelly enquired.

"Long morning," she said.

"Yeah, know the feeling love. Well, I better get back to the station in case there has been a robbery or something important that needs the full attention of the law."

He tapped the desk, gave Michael a passing nod without really seeing him, and tucked his losing ticket safely into his shirt pocket again.

"Next time," he told the room. "I'm backing the ugly one at the long odds. Seems to be the go."

The door chimed as he left.

CHAPTER 16

COUNTING THE COST

Brisbane, late 1992

For a few seconds, nobody moved.

Outside, the police car's indicator ticked and Donnelly pulled away.

Hazel's knees dipped. She caught herself on the counter, feeling every year in her bones.

"He didn't know," Michael said. His voice sounded stunned more than relieved. "He was right there and he didn't know."

"Cops see what they expect to see," Angus said. "He came in for a flutter and a chat, not a bust. World's full of people missing the obvious."

Claire let out a shaky laugh that wasn't really a laugh.

"He asked me how I was," she said. "I nearly told him I'd just watched my life flash past my eyes while a shotgun waved at my head."

Michael's gaze dropped to the worn carpet, his whole posture deflated, as if he'd finally run out of excuses for himself.

"I wasn't going to hurt anyone," he said quickly. "I swear to God, I wasn't."

"That's not the point, love," Hazel replied, softer than she meant to. "We all had a front-row seat to what could've happened."

Charlie dragged a hand down his face.

"I kept thinking he'd smell it," he said. "Like he'd take one look at us and say, 'Right, everyone against the wall'. I couldn't even look at him properly. I thought if I met his eyes, I'd just confess to things I haven't even done yet."

"You should try the things I have done," Angus muttered. "His hand was on that radio the whole time. One twitch and we're all in the back of a divvy van arguing over whose stupid idea this was."

Michael stared at his own hands, as if checking they were still attached.

"I thought … when he walked in … that this was the part where it all ends," he said. "Daniela on her own. Me explaining this to my mum and dad from behind glass. The whole lot."

Hazel felt a sting behind her eyes and blinked it away.

"Well, lucky it didn't," she said. "Somehow, we just sold the most obvious mess in Brisbane as a normal mid-week afternoon."

"Doesn't feel normal," Claire whispered. "My legs are still jelly. I don't know how I'm supposed to go back to life tomorrow and pretend this was just another day."

Charlie gave a small, brittle nod.

"We're all going to have to pretend," he said. "Feels like … maybe for the rest of our lives."

Hazel straightened a fraction, pushing the tremor down. The fear could wait; the decisions couldn't.

"We've got a big win with a lot of strings attached," she went on. "We have to get Angus's ticket and whatever payout we're allowed to touch in a way that doesn't ring every bell from here to Alice Springs."

She looked at Angus, then Charlie, then Michael and Claire.

"Start talking, Scotsman," she said. "Because whatever we do from here on in, we can't afford to be as stupid as we were brave."

"Well, we've just turned your last twenty into an amount even Craig couldn't calculate," Angus said.

"Charlie, what are we talking here, how much?" Hazel asked. "Give me a ballpark. And don't be generous with the rounding."

Charlie rubbed his forehead.

He looked up at the odds graphic still glowing in the corner of the TV, then hesitated, as if saying it out loud might make it vanish.

"Twenty grand at seventy-one-to-one," he said. "That's probably around one point four million. Now take out Mac's clip, and Hazel's up-front cash, maybe there is a million left for all of us to share."

Michael swayed.

San Diego stepped out of the realm of glossy brochures and into something that looked uncomfortably like an invoice with numbers he could, in theory, pay with his share.

He pictured Daniela's face at their wedding, confetti in her hair. Her fingers on the IVF pamphlets spread across their kitchen table. The day the specialist had said we're running out of options; for the first time since, the future didn't feel like a slammed door.

Hazel's stomach jolted. The figure was too big and too small at the same time. Enough to change things. Not enough to erase the way they'd got it.

"So what happens now?" she asked. "Walk me through how a man like Macready handles this, and don't sugarcoat it."

Angus scratched at his beard.

"Mac's already got his hooks deep in multiple payout streams from that race," he said. "He had people like me putting money on Trimax from different holes in the wall so it didn't all smell like the same pocket. Our call from here, plus whatever went on in person, plus blokes on other phones … that's how the odds shifted late."

"And our bit?" Charlie asked.

"Officially, that twenty was just another river connecting to the ocean," Angus said. "It's sitting under an account he arranged out there. Mac will have his own lad collect the bulk. Some of it will disappear straight into his account for whatever he's propping up this month, loans, debts, favours. The rest …"

He gave Hazel a look.

"The rest … well, that is now what he owes me … owes us I meant. He'll expect me to take that slice and not ask any questions."

Claire rubbed her temples.

"So, we just sit back and let the beast feed itself whatever it desires and accept the leftovers?" Claire enquired.

"Precisely, the last thing we all need is that beast called Macready coming to us looking for an even bigger meal," Angus confirmed.

Charlie's brain latched onto that.

"What does 'feed the beast' mean in numbers?" he asked.

Angus thought for a second. "He won't blink at carving out, say, a third as his," he said. "Might be more, might be less. He won't be sending us a profit-and-loss statement I can guarantee you that, Rain-Man."

"Angus," Hazel interjected. "That's not called for. Remember our pact? We are in this together, and Charlie is just asking a fair question."

"Sorry Charlie. But if I push back even a little, he'll smell it. We're better off letting him think he's done very nicely and quietly working with the leftovers together."

Claire let out a slow breath.

"So, the first cost of our miracle," she said, "is that a professional criminal gets richer and we pretend that's just fine."

"Compared to his usual clients," Angus said, "we're getting a bargain."

Nobody laughed.

"Alright," Charlie said. "Leave him his cut. What about the part that comes back to us? We can't all stroll into any bank with empty suitcases and come home smiling."

"Jesus, no," Angus said. "Mac would have a fit if he saw us anywhere near the big payout. That bit stays in his channels. What he'll do, what he normally does, is let some of it trickle back to me through a separate line. Smaller amounts, over time. Different shapes. That way it looks legit on the surface."

"Well, that's settled, we're not walking out of here today as millionaires," Michael said.

"Definitely not," Hazel replied. "We're walking out of here today with a horrible secret, and a promise from a criminal. The money's in the post, if we're lucky."

The honesty steadied her.

"What are we talking here then Angus, weeks, maybe months?"

"At least," Angus said. "Slow and boring is good. It's safe. Celebrate the small amounts, the little wins."

Charlie's shoulders eased a fraction. Processes. He could almost see a workflow. "And when it lands?" he asked. "We need rules. Otherwise, this becomes the thing that eats us."

Hazel nodded.

"The rules haven't changed," she said. "We made them before Angus picked up that phone."

She ticked them off on her fingers.

"One: the robbery money is already back where it belongs. The fake shotgun, crowbar, balaclava and duffle bag go home with Angus for appropriate disposal. Somewhere never to be found again. This shop's till balances tonight. On paper, nothing was taken."

Michael glanced at the counter, specifically at the till, and what could have been.

"Two," Hazel went on. "Whatever Angus manages to get out of Macready's channels, we split the way we said. First, the bank and anyone with an invoice in Jim's pile, they all get what's needed so they stop owning me."

She took a breath.

"After that, Michael gets enough to trek over to San Diego and pay for whatever chance there is."

Michael opened his mouth, then shut it again. The word 'chance' brought him back to reality.

"Claire, Charlie, Angus? Any dreams, for yourself, or others?"

Claire stared at the floor for a long moment.

Her patients' faces drifted up; kids with drip stands and teddy bears. Parents needing to be brave for everyone else.

"I don't want anything immediately for myself," Claire said at last. "I'm certainly not the ex-doctor who used dirty money to buy a fancy car to compensate for everything else I stuffed up recently in life."

Charlie swallowed.

"I would love to set up a fund. Quietly. Something that helps families who have to travel to the city for treatment. Petrol. Motels. Meals that aren't from vending machines. They shouldn't have to choose between being there to support a loved one or paying the bills."

Silence stretched for a moment.

Charlie broke it, voice low.

"If my father ever finds out the full story at work, or even half of it, he'll cut me off from the family trust," he said. "He's been looking for an excuse anyway. Says I rely on it too much."

Hazel watched him, seeing the careful shirt, the good watch, the lines of strain at the corners of his eyes.

"My wife's used to a certain way of living," Charlie went on. "Country clubs, holidays that come with little chocolates on the pillow. If he pulls the plug, I either learn how to pay for that life myself or I watch it all go, including her."

He gave a small, humourless smile.

"I don't want a faster boat or a different colour sports car. I just want a buffer. Something put away, quiet and boring. Call it an exit fund, if I need it."

Hazel nodded once. It was logical, and foolish at the same time; wanting to keep a marriage afloat, by continuing to reward the behaviour that was possibly tearing it apart.

"And you, Angus?" she asked. "What does 'leftovers' look like in your world?"

Angus turned his head to look outside the front door, searching for horizons only a life lived on the dark side could see.

"I've spent most of my life waiting for the knock at the door," he said. "Always owed someone. Always one mistake away from going back inside."

He scratched at his beard again.

"I've got a sister back in Glasgow, raising her grandkids on whatever the government throws her way," he said. "One of the boys is getting old enough now that the streets are starting to notice him. I'd like to send something over regular, not once in a blue moon when I've had a good run."

He cleared his throat.

"And closer to home … I wouldn't mind buying myself out of a few old promises. Pay back some people who helped me when they shouldn't have. Set up a little place that's mine proper. Maybe a workshop, maybe a tiny flat that no one can take because I missed a payment. Somewhere I'm not living out of a bag or on someone's goodwill."

He shrugged, suddenly awkward.

"Nothing flash. Just enough that when I finally hang up my boots, I'm not doing it in a cell or under a bridge."

Hazel let their wishes hang in the air for a moment. A motel room for a sick kid's parents, a marriage propped up when the trust fund dried, a Scottish boy kept off a corner, an ex-con with a front door that locked from the inside. All felt like wholesale outcomes from a batch of dirty money.

"Then that's it," she said. "You all give me your phone numbers; we lock up and go home. Tomorrow, we get on with our lives again and we do not flinch if, and when, we cross paths with each other again."

She turned to Angus, expression sharpening.

"And if anyone gets clever ideas about changing our agreed plans or breaking the sacred pact, you can expect a visit from Angus and a few of his boys."

Angus nodded.

"We shall call it gentle persuasion, Hazel" he stated in a calm, but equally terrifying tone.

Michael took a big gulp of air.

CHAPTER 17

LOCKING UP

Brisbane, late 1992

The rest of the afternoon blurred into ordinary situations. The printer coughed out tickets. Coins clinked in the till. Someone laughed too loudly at another punter's misfortune, from near the form guides. A race caller waffled on about rail positions and track firmness. Normality crept back in.

Hazel let it.

A couple of regulars drifted in, oblivious to the fact that the place had almost become a crime scene twice over. She welcomed them, took their small bets, handed back change.

Only once did her fingers truly shake, when a stranger wandered in and asked for a single dollar on the nose of a seventy-to-one greyhound going around in race 7 at Dapto. Eventually she saw the funny side of this ironic circumstance.

Michael hovered near the wall, pretending to study a form guide he wasn't reading. To anyone who glanced at him he was just another punter killing time. To Hazel, every stiff movement he made screamed 'don't look too closely'.

He tried to focus on the names and numbers on the page. They blurred. All he could see were other lines: account balances, airfare prices, clinic invoices, the costs of the San Diego procedure he'd worn a balaclava to try achieve.

He pictured walking back through his front door. Daniela would be in the kitchen or on the couch, a magazine open, pretending not to be counting the days and months between appointments.

What do you say after a day like this? Traffic was bad. Job ran over. I pointed a fake gun at a woman you'd probably like, and we all bet your future on a crooked horse race.

If the money never landed, if Macready vanished, or Angus misjudged him, or some clerk in Alice Springs smelled a rat; then this could be the day he'd taken far too great a risk for no return.

When the room thinned and no one stood at the counter, he moved towards the counter.

Hazel kept her eyes on the till, tapping keys she didn't need to tap.

"Go," she murmured, not looking up. "And don't turn around at the window. People who look back get remembered."

He hesitated. She could feel his stare on the top of her head. Then the door clicked, and a slice of traffic noise cut through the shop.

She watched his reflection instead – a tall shape in the glass, shoulders hunched, striding across the car park like any other bloke coming to terms with a bad day on the punt.

Michael reached his car and gripped the steering wheel before he even sat down. He started the car and left.

Angus left next, after making a show of putting a small, harmless bet on a mid-week trotter in Sydney. He leaned on the counter as if nothing more serious than form lines weighed on him.

"I'll make the calls I need to make," he said quietly. "Not tonight. Soon. We'll keep it all under the radar."

"That would be nice," Hazel said.

Angus threw the duffle bag and its unwanted contents over his shoulder like he was about to head to the gym.

"I'll get rid of this thing properly," he added. "No souvenirs."

"See that you do," she said. "I don't want to read about some kid finding it in a creek."

"Slow and boring," he said, more to himself than to Hazel. "That's the dream, eh?"

He nodded to Claire and Charlie and wandered out into the fading light, just another rough-edged man stepping back into the world with more on his mind than he'd ever say.

Claire stayed longer.

She perched on a stool near the end of the counter, jacket still around her shoulders, fingers wrapped around a cup of bad coffee Hazel had produced from the back.

Her hands wanted a drink that came from a bottle, not a kettle. But she knew exactly where that road led.

"You alright to get home?" Hazel asked.

"I've survived night shifts in emergency on less," Claire said. "I'll get a cab. I'm not trusting myself on another Brisbane bus today."

She chuckled.

In her head, she could already hear what her next AA meeting should sound like.

"Hi, I'm Claire and I'm an alcoholic, and an ex-doctor that now helps launder the proceeds of fixed races for criminals."

"Thank you," Claire said, "For not letting me die and for whatever this whole event was."

"It was madness," Hazel said. "But it was … considered madness, eventually."

She glanced around the shop, the posters, the scuffed plastic chairs, the glow of the screens. All the places her legs had nearly given way.

"You going to be okay here?" Claire asked.

"Better than I was," Hazel said. "Owing less hopefully, at least in dollars."

Claire nodded once, as if Hazel had given a clinical update that satisfied her.

She squeezed Hazel's forearm briefly, and left without looking back, already rehearsing tomorrow's meeting in her head, the parts she could say.

Charlie lingered until close.

He fussed with a biro near the form guides, pretending to make notes. When the last regular shuffled out and the door chimed shut behind him, Charlie walked up to the counter.

"Today was … a statistical outlier," he said.

Hazel snorted.

"That's one way of putting it."

They stood in companionable silence for a moment, watching the TV run through a replay of a race they didn't care about.

For Charlie, the real replay was still going in his head: Donnelly's uniform at the counter, Angus talking about feeding beasts, the moment Charlie had done the mental arithmetic and realised how big, and how impossible, the win really was.

He could already feel tomorrow pressing in. The mahogany boardroom. His boss asking where Charlie had disappeared to yesterday afternoon when he'd been needed on a call to discuss his father's questionable business dealings.

If the money came through, it would be his buffer. The thing that meant when, not if, his father finally cut the trust fund strings, his whole life wouldn't fall into a heap. He could keep a roof over his family's head long enough until he worked out who he was without leveraging the Hinton family name.

If it didn't? Then he'd have a secret for nothing and one more weight on his conscience.

As he walked out, Charlie was already rehearsing lies that sounded like sensible explanations. If anyone ever noticed an odd deposit down the track, he'd have a story prepared, an old investment, a side deal, anything but the truth: I once split a dirty miracle with four strangers.

Eventually, it was just Hazel.

She closed the last cash drawer, wrote the numbers she needed to write, made sure every slip and docket sat where it ought to. The balances matched. On paper, it had been a strange day, but not an impossible one. No robbery. No windfall. Just turnover and petty wins and losses.

The lie of normality was neat. Too neat.

She thought of the weeks ahead. Donnelly could wander back in any time, wanting another flutter, and her heart would try to punch its way out of her chest. Craig could turn up with that oily smile and a new 'opportunity', still thinking she was cornered. The bank could send another letter, dates and threats neatly typed.

She would have to stand here, day after day, smiling at pensioners and tradies, knowing the floor had once held a man in a balaclava and the air had once tasted like pure fear. She'd have to pretend her life was as simple as 'first past the post' when the truth was now buried under favours and fixed odds.

At the alarm panel near the door, she hesitated.

The plastic cover hung crooked. Wires poked out where Jim had once tried to fix it himself, declaring that any electrician who charged those rates was a thief. He'd tapped the panel, grinned at her, and said, "No one's that interested in our little shop, love. Crim's have got bigger fish to fry."

The world had taken a bite today.

Maybe, it was time those wires were finally sorted by someone who knew what they were doing. Maybe it was time her life wasn't built on favours and half-fixes and letting men with slick voices call her 'girl' and talk her into corners.

Tomorrow, it begins.

She flicked the switch she did have. The one that cut the lights. The TAB dropped into a softer gloom, lit only by the glow from the passing traffic.

Hazel stepped outside, pulled the glass door shut, and locked it. She tested the handle twice. Habit.

The sky over Gympie Road was bruised purple, the typical Brisbane summer storm on the way. Hazel Andrews walked to the bus stop with her nylon bag and twenty thousand dollars still intact.

As she took her seat on the Council bus, she thought about the horse Trimax and her four new acquaintances.

Hazel didn't know who any of them could become in the future. She only knew that Race 7 was over.

But the real finish line remained out there in the distance; unwritten and uncalled.

CHAPTER 18

THE AFTERMATH

Brisbane, late 1993

Michael,

You're probably surprised to see my name again.

I found your postal address in the white pages. I know it is sneaky, but I figured that after you waved a shotgun in my shop, we could call it even.

It's been almost two years since you walked into the Aspley TAB. I still don't like thinking about it, but here we are.

Time blurs the edges if you let it. I can still see the important bits clearly enough: your hands shaking; Claire on the floor; Angus swearing under his breath; Charlie doing sums in his head; me with a gun at my shoulder I had no business holding.

Most days now, it feels like something that happened to other people in another suburb. Then I hear a race call and my stomach remembers before my head does.

You're going to open this and go straight to the cheque, so let's get that out of the way.

Yes, it's real. Yes, it's your share.

No, it isn't a trick, and no, you are not to come anywhere near me to say, 'thank you'.

The amount will probably make you go a bit quiet. It made me sit down.

If you're wondering whether I was tempted to keep it, the answer is yes. Briefly. Then I remembered what it was for, and who you were when you told me.

You said 'San Diego' like it was another planet. I've never been further than the Gold Coast. To me it's a name on a brochure. To you it's the last gate between the life you've got and the one you wanted.

I haven't forgotten your wife's face when you spoke about her, even with that wool thing over your head. I haven't forgotten the way your voice cracked when you said you were out of options.

So here it is. One last option.

I want to be very clear: this money is dirty. We both know that. It came from a fake gun, a fixed race, and a day none of us would repeat for anything.

You don't clean that by putting it in a nice envelope and calling it 'a chance'. But you can decide what you do with it now.

I'm sending it because I don't want that day to be the full stop on your life. I'm also sending it because I don't want you anywhere near whatever is left of mine.

That's the bargain.

Practicalities, because that's the bit that actually matters.

The cheque is drawn on an account that doesn't have my name or yours on it. Angus organised that through one of his ex-mates who still answers when he rings. Don't ask for details; you don't need them and I don't want them in my head.

You should be able to put it into whatever account you like without too many questions, as long as you don't wave it around. Pay clinic invoices. Pay for plane tickets. Pay rent if you need to. Don't buy a boat. I mean that.

As for the rest of us, because I know you'll wonder, here's what that horse and that crazy afternoon has done.

I paid out what Jim owed, on paper and in my head. The shop stopped feeling like a ransom note from past mistakes. The bank manager's voice went from 'final notice' to 'we can work with this' quicker than I expected. I cleared the loans on the house and it finally felt like mine, not part of Jim's mess.

Before I sold the place, there was a strange stretch of months where life looked almost ordinary again, if you didn't look too hard at the foundations. The TAB went back to being the same old hope trap on Gympie Road, the cost of bad decisions etched into customers' faces.

Every so often, Charlie would appear on the footpath across the road. For a while it was just him, suit jacket off, tie loosened, walking too fast like he was trying to outpace a thought. Later, he had company.

The first time I saw the pram I didn't recognise him. Just another young dad, pushing something expensive with his whole body tilted forward like he was trying not to roll backwards down a hill of responsibility. Then his wife came into view, polished, put-together, the way he'd described without meaning to when he talked about 'little chocolates on the pillow'.

And then I saw them: twin girls, one in the pram, one holding his hand and tugging towards the newsagent window, wanting to press her nose to the glass and look inside.

He always hesitated for half a second when TAB came into his line of sight. Once, he did come in. Left the pram and his wife outside, ducked through the door on some excuse about needing change. He put twenty on something short-priced, said, "How's business?" like it was a test. I said, "Ticking over," and handed him his ticket. Neither of us mentioned Race 7.

Mostly, though, he walked by. I like to think his share of the money turned into sensible, boring things, a different mortgage that was in his name, school-fee plans, a buffer so that when his father finally *made good on those threats about cutting him off, his whole life didn't sink in one go. If that's how it went, then I suppose Trimax bought two little girls a slightly safer childhood, in between all the rubbish.*

Angus was different.

For a while, he used to pop in once a month or so, always at odd times. He'd stand at the counter with a Trading Post rolled in his big hand, like a man who'd wandered in by habit more than intention.

"How's the beast?" I'd ask, meaning Macready and his world.

"Fed and sleeping," he'd say, if things were quiet. Other times he'd just grunt and ask for a small bet on some horse no one else was touching, more superstition than investment.

Out the back, over cheap tea, he let slip little bits of what he'd done with his cut. Nothing too detailed; years in his line of work teach you how to talk in suggestions, not specifics. But I know this much: some of it went back to Glasgow, regular envelopes instead of occasional scraps. His sister's grandkids apparently had new school shoes and a heater that worked more often than it didn't.

Closer to home, he mentioned renting a tiny flat that was his, proper lease and all. No more crashing in other people's spare rooms between jobs. He talked about a shed somewhere in a light industrial strip where he could tinker with things he probably shouldn't name, but from the way his shoulders eased when he spoke about it, I got the sense it was the closest thing he'd ever had to a hobby.

Then, one day, he stopped appearing.

No quick bets on midweek dogs, no cups of tea, no heavy footsteps at the back door. Nothing.

I'd like to tell you I investigated. I didn't. In his world, asking too many questions is its own kind of danger. I did think about it, though, every time a news report mentioned a drug bust or a gang fight or 'an unnamed man in his forties or fifties' and didn't show a face.

There's a chance he skipped town, found himself another beast to feed somewhere else. There's a chance he annoyed the wrong person and ended up in a ditch. There's another, very real chance he's back inside, counting the days in a place he knows too well.

If he is in jail, I suppose one small mercy is that he'll be the only bloke in his unit with enough tucked away somewhere for decent supply of Tally-Ho papers and tobacco. It's a small comfort, but men like Angus take them where they can.

Claire, you'll want to know about her.

Her share went into that fund she talked about. She didn't just shove it into a biscuit tin and hope for the best. She did it properly, registered a name, got an ABN, sat in an accountant's office filling out forms until she wanted to scream. She sent me a copy of the paperwork like a kid bringing home a good report card.

There's a letter from the hospital pinned to my fridge. Under all the long words the gist was simple: because of 'the fund', families from out west have petrol to get here and somewhere half-decent to sleep when their kids need treatment. Someone gets to sit at a bedside without calculating every kilometre in their head.

Claire has gone back to study nursing. She told me once, over the phone, that she wanted to 'do it as the person I am now, not the mess I used to be'. I didn't ask whether she meant the drinking or the things we did with Trimax. Maybe both.

So that's them.

As for me; after the debts were cleared and the screams in my head got a little quieter, I sold the shop.

You'd probably laugh if you saw the bloke who bought it. Cashed up from down the coast, thinks he's going to semi-retire on quaddies and quick-pick multis. I hope the place is kinder to him than it was to me, but part of me suspects the TAB will simply be itself, no matter who's got their name on the shop front.

I walked out of there with a clean name, a modest balance, and a set of keys that no longer rattled like a life sentence. I bought a small unit, where the roof doesn't leak when it storms and there's a tree outside *the window instead of Gympie Road.*

I also bought some canvas and a small box of oils.

Don't get excited. I'm not announcing a great artistic comeback. I set up a card table by the window and make a mess that smells like turps. Most of it is rubbish. That's fine. It's mine. Every now and then, a shape turns up on the canvas that looks like something I meant, not just a smear. On good days, I think Jim would have liked that. On bad ones, I'm just glad my hands are busy with something other than betting tickets and debt letters.

Now the part you'll want to argue with.

Do not write back.

Do not come to wherever you think I might be living now. Do not send flowers or bottles or anything else you think might stand in for thanks.

You said once you never wanted to see my face in a courtroom. I feel the same way about yours in my doorway.

We don't owe each other friendship. We don't even really owe each other kindness beyond what we've done here. We were five people in the wrong place at the wrong time who did something mad and lucky and terrible together.

That's a kind of bond, but it's not the sort you build a life around.

If your wife asks where the money came from, tell her whatever you can live with. Call it an old investment coming good, a forgotten policy, a relative who finally did something useful. Or tell her the truth, if you think your marriage is made of sturdier stuff than mine was. That's your business.

Just don't use my name in the story.

I'd rather be the cranky woman who ran the Aspley TAB than a supporting character in some tidy little story with enough detail for someone to put a face to my name.

You might think I'm being cold. I think this is me being as fair as I know how.

You came into my life with a weapon and a plan that didn't include anyone else making it home unchanged. You walked out with more than you deserved and, somehow, so did I. Between those two points I did things I'll have to live with. So did you.

I'm giving you this because we agreed it was the only way any of this had a chance of meaning something other than a police report and traumatic memories. I'm also drawing a line.

Take the money. Get yourselves to San Diego. Pay whoever needs paying. Sit in whatever waiting rooms you have to sit in. If some doctor in a white coat in a place I'll never see tells you there's a real chance, take it.

If things go your way and there's a baby at the end of all this, I hope they never see a room like my TAB. I hope they grow up thinking racehorses are just animals on TV other people shout at. I hope their biggest worry is who forgot to pack the orange slices for soccer.

If things don't go your way, and sometimes they don't, no matter how hard you push, then at least you'll know you tried everything. You won't be forty-five, staring at the ceiling at three in the morning, wondering what else you could have done.

Either way, the story between you and me ends with this envelope.

Money doesn't fix the past. It just gives you better choices for what to do next.

You've got one now. Use it.

I now understand that true fear doesn't vanish, but it does shrink if you stop feeding it.

Hazel Andrews
(formerly of the Aspley TAB)

CHAPTER 19

THE BIRTHDAY CONFESSION

Brisbane, early 1994

Over a year had passed since the robbery in Aspley, and almost three months since the cheque arrived in the post with Hazel's tight, uncompromising letter also enclosed.

Michael often woke with the TAB featuring in his dream, feeling the dull ache of a hangover without the alcohol.

Today was his birthday. Thirty.

'Congratulations,' he thought, dragging a shirt over his head. Three decades in, and he still couldn't manage basic accountability for his own choices.

"Don't be late," Daniela had said the night before, leaning in the bathroom doorway while he spat toothpaste into the sink. "Breakfast, remember? I booked somewhere special. No arguments."

He'd tried to smile around the foam.

"Wouldn't dream of it," he'd said.

The café she picked had big bay windows and too many pot plants. He spotted her through the glass before he reached the door.

She'd claimed a table by the window. A single helium balloon bobbed above her chair; a gaudy '30' he wanted to swat away. There was a stack of pancakes in front of his place with a candle stuck in the top one, waiting to be lit.

She'd also ordered his coffee. He could see the flat white, steaming gently, one sugar packet torn open and waiting beside the saucer.

Daniela looked up as the bell on the door chimed. Her face lit.

"Happy birthday," she said, standing to kiss his cheek.

He kissed her back, awkward, too aware of the distance that had crept in over the past year.

"Thanks," he said, sitting opposite.

She'd made an effort. Hair done. Nice top. Lipstick. She looked like the woman he'd married, sitting across the table from a man she wasn't sure about anymore.

"Make a wish," she said, lighting the candle. "Then blow it out before it burns the place down."

He stared at the tiny flame.

'Don't let this destroy everything', he thought. Then he blew.

The smoke curled up between them. She clapped quietly, smiled, then watched him in that way that made him feel like an endangered specimen in the zoo.

"You're quiet," she said. "Even for you."

"I'm fine," he lied. "Just … thirty."

"You've been weird for months," she said. "It's not just turning thirty."

He pushed his fork through the top pancake, cutting a wedge he couldn't imagine swallowing.

"It's work," he said automatically, the old, safe excuse.

"No," she said. "It's not."

He looked up.

"Is there someone else?" she asked. No drama. Just a woman

who'd rehearsed the question in her head for days and finally let it out.

He recoiled.

"No," he said quickly. "No. Nothing like that. It's … worse. And dumber."

He watched the colour shift in her face, a shade at a time.

"Start at the start," she said. "Use small words."

He swallowed.

"Around twelve months ago," he said, "I walked into a TAB at Aspley with a shotgun and a bag."

She stared at him.

For a second she didn't react at all. He watched the information stack up behind her eyes, piece by piece.

"You're kidding," she said at last.

He rubbed a hand over his face, as if he could wipe his poor decision away.

"Please tell me you're joking," she said. "Because that's not … that's not a joke, Michael."

He looked at her and didn't say anything. Let the silence answer.

Her hand went to her mouth.

"Oh, my God," she whispered. "You're serious."

The café noise fell away. Plates clinking, coffee machine hissing, someone's toddler complaining about burnt toast all disappeared.

"Why?" she asked eventually. "Why on earth would you do something like that?"

"Because we needed the money," he said. The words sounded pathetic even to him. "It was more than we could save in time. I couldn't see another way."

Her eyes flashed.

"So, you picked up a gun," she said. "You, the man who almost cries when you accidentally stand on a dog's tail. You believed the best solution was … armed robbery?"

"I wasn't thinking straight," he said. "I was thinking about you. About San Diego. About the way you looked at babies in prams when you thought I wasn't watching."

"You were thinking about yourself," she said quietly. "About not feeling like a failure."

He opened his mouth, then closed it again. She wasn't wrong.

"I thought," he said slowly, "if I came home with the money, it would fix things. Or at least give us a real chance."

She stared at him, breathing carefully through her nose.

"And this shotgun," she said. "Where did you get it?"

"A bloke I knew from … before," he said. "He arranged it. A favour."

She watched him like she was watching a stranger narrate a nightmare.

"Was it loaded?" she asked.

He remembered the weight of it in his hands, the way everyone's faces had changed when he'd pulled it from the bag. The way his own stomach had dropped.

"No," he said. "It wasn't loaded. It wasn't even … real. Just an old replica. No firing pin. It looked scary, but it couldn't have done anything."

The words tasted like spin even as he said them. He watched them land on her face, saw the way her eyes narrowed.

"You're sure," she said.

"Positive," he said. "I'm not … I'm not that person, Dani. I was stupid and reckless, but I wasn't planning to actually hurt anyone."

"You terrified a room full of people," she said, "with a fake gun, for our family."

"Yes," he said.

It was easier to own that version than the one where an ex-doctor collapsed, a racehorse in the desert ran exactly the way it was told to by a criminal network, and everyone walked away with grime on their conscience and money in their pockets.

"Did anyone get hurt?" she asked.

"No," he said quickly. That part, at least, was true. "No. I dropped the gun. The woman behind the counter … she took it off me. Nobody was physically hurt."

"Physically," she repeated.

He winced.

"They were frightened," he said. "Obviously. I was frightened. I wanted to throw up the whole time. It was the stupidest thing I've ever done."

"Not disagreeing," she said.

Her hands were shaking now. She put them in her lap, out of sight.

"And this woman," she went on. "The one at the counter. She just … what? Let you walk out?"

"Not exactly," he said.

He told her, haltingly, about one of the other customers naming a race in Alice Springs. About a horse called Trimax that was never meant to lose. About four strangers in a shabby suburban TAB making a pact in the ten minutes between races.

He didn't go into detail about the enforcer in the desert or the phone calls. Those parts were too hard to explain without everything unravelling into something even uglier.

He did tell her about the cheque.

"Months later," he said, "the woman from the TAB wrote to me. Sent my share. Said it was the only way to make that day mean anything other than what we'd done."

He slid his fingers over the placemat, tracing a coffee stain.

"She made rules," he went on. "Paid out what needed paying. Cleared her debts. Sent me enough to get us to San Diego and try again. And a letter that basically said, 'Don't come near me, and don't ever use my name in the story'."

Daniela looked out the window, grinding her teeth.

People walked past with shopping bags. A kid dragged his scooter along the pavement and demanded lollies from his parents. The world did not care that her marriage had just shifted on its foundations.

"Do you know how many times I sat in that clinic," she said, "holding your hand, thinking we're the good ones?"

He winced.

"Good people," she went on, her voice flat. "Doing our best. Playing by the rules. I thought if we just kept showing up, the universe would stop picking on us. I told myself you were doing everything you could."

"I was," he said. "I am. This … was my horrible, desperate version of 'everything'."

"You lied," she said simply.

He had no answer to that.

They sat in thick silence. The candle burned down to a stub, wax pooling in the holder.

"I don't even know what I'm meant to feel," she said eventually. "Part of me wants to ring my parents. Part of me wants to walk out and never see you again. Part of me wants to throw this plate at your head."

She let out a brittle laugh that had no joy in it.

"I am so sorry," he said.

It sounded small.

She didn't say, "I forgive you." She didn't say, "Get out."

She stared at him like she could see every bad decision layered over his face.

"Do the police know?" she asked at last. "Has anyone … come after you?"

"No," he said. "All those were sorted. As long as I keep my

mouth shut and stay away from everyone."

"And if someone does come knocking?" she said.

"Then I tell the truth," he said. "Properly. To whoever's asking. I'm done with hiding. Hence …" He gestured at the table, the balloon, the cold pancakes. "This."

She nodded once.

"I need time," she said. "To think. To be angry. To work out if I can look at you without seeing … that shotgun."

"I understand," he said.

"No, you don't," she retaliated. "But you can start by not trying to fix it in one conversation."

He shut his mouth.

She picked up her bag, then paused.

"I organised all this because I wanted today to be … hopeful," she said. "New decade. New year, new chances. I thought maybe the worst was behind us."

She gave a small, humourless snort.

"Turns out I'd already been living in the worst without realising," she said. "That's a handy thing to know."

She stood.

"Are you coming home?" he asked, hating how tentative he sounded.

"Eventually," she said. "But not with you. Not right now. I'm going to Mum's. I need to work out whether I'm married to my husband or just … someone I used to share everything with over coffee."

He nodded. He couldn't blame her; it was exactly how he'd felt about himself for months.

She walked out, leaving him and the balloon bobbing over an empty chair.

CHAPTER 20

THE UNEXPECTED CALL

Brisbane, mid-1995

Daniela sat in her car outside Woolworths Coorparoo with both hands on the steering wheel, watching people come and go.

A woman wrangled two kids into a trolley. A man in a hi-vis shirt shoved a slab of soft drink into his boot. A teenager leaned against a post, smoking like he was in a film.

The shopping list on the passenger seat had two different handwritings. Her neat capitals. Michael's rushed scrawl on the bottom from two weeks ago, back when they still wrote lists together instead of sticking Post-It Notes on each other's bedroom doors.

She flipped it over, so she didn't have to look at it.

She'd been sleeping in the spare room since his birthday.

Four months of surface-level politeness.

"Can you pass the salt?"

"I'll be late tonight."

"Did you feed the dog?"

Her mouth remembered how to say words; her body learned how to stand near him without feeling anything.

When he finally owned up to what he'd done, he'd looked so small across that café table. It had almost broken her. Almost. Survival instinct had refused to let empathy drown out her fury.

She'd stayed. That surprised her as much as his confession. Whatever mix of love, history and sheer stubbornness existed, it hadn't let her walk out.

Daniela grabbed the list, shoved it into her handbag and went inside. There were still dinners to cook and milk to buy, whether your husband had confessed to armed robbery or not.

By the time she wrestled the shopping bags into the kitchen, the house felt too quiet.

Michael's car wasn't in the driveway. His boots weren't by the door. He'd told her the night before, careful, like asking permission. "I'll stay at Mum's tonight," he'd said. "Give you space. I'll be back tomorrow before work."

She'd nodded, throat tight. Space had become their default setting.

She unpacked the bags on autopilot. Bread in the bread bin. Fruit into the bowl that had once held congratulations cards. Milk in the fridge next to a half-empty bottle of white wine she was trying not to make a habit of.

The phone rang.

For a second she thought about letting it ring out. The machine would get it. Probably her mother-in-law, or a friend wanting to 'just check in' in a tone that made her want to pull the entire phone from the wall and throw it at the floor.

She sighed, sat down and picked it up.

"Hello?"

"Mrs Whelan?" The voice was professional, careful. "This is Sarah from the Brisbane Fertility Centre."

Daniela felt like the floor shifted half an inch.

"I … we're not … Michael and I aren't exactly … in a great place to be talking about treatment right now," she launched straight in; well before a reciprocal 'hello' had entered her thought process.

"Oh, okay. Sorry to hear that, Daniela. I understand the timing may be difficult," the woman said gently. "I'm calling because we've recently expanded our donor program, and your file was one of the ones we selected for consideration."

Daniela's sat up in the chair; the wobbly one Michael had been promising to fix since last Christmas.

"A donor," she said.

"Yes," Sarah replied. "Someone has come forward specifically wanting to help a couple whose infertility isn't straightforward. Dr Jonze felt your situation might align with the donor's wishes."

'Our situation', Daniela thought bitterly. Infertile husband. Still-no-baby. Several rounds of 'we're so sorry, not this time' later. Oh, and throw in a failed robbery attempt nobody at the clinic knew about.

"While we're not privy to all your personal circumstances beyond the medical notes," Sarah went on. "We do see from your file that you've been through a lot. I'm very sorry those attempts didn't result in a pregnancy."

Daniela pressed her palm flat on the table. The laminate was warm from the afternoon sun.

"This donor," she said quietly. "Why? Why would someone do this?"

"People have all kinds of reasons," Sarah said. "Sometimes they've experienced infertility in a different configuration. Some-times they've lost pregnancies; sometimes they've decided not to have children but want to help others. In this case, the donor has specifically asked to be matched with a couple who've had a difficult journey because of circumstances beyond their control. That described your file."

Daniela blinked.

Because of circumstances outside their control.

Circumstances like a broken engineer with blocked tubes. Circumstances like a widow in Aspley refusing to let that be their story and sending a cheque in the mail.

"In one sense," she said, more to herself than to Sarah, "nothing's changed in our world since we sadly discovered infertility was going to be a part of our journey. We haven't had the energy to think about making babies."

"Well, this provides a different pathway that you may have yet considered. It won't be right for everyone. But we wanted you to have the option to come in and talk it through properly if any interest exists."

"What if my partner doesn't want to come?" Daniela asked. The word husband felt too fragile. "What if he's not … up for that conversation?"

"It's not uncommon for couples to be at different stages," Sarah replied. "You're welcome to attend an information session on your own. We can talk through medical and emotional considerations. No decisions have to be made that day."

Just her. Not them. Not at the moment anyway.

"Yes," Daniela heard herself say. "Just me."

"Alright," Sarah said. "We have an opening next Thursday at ten, or the following Monday at four."

"Thursday," Daniela said quickly. If she thought about it too long, she might curl up on the spare-room bed and ruminate.

They settled details; time, paperwork, what to bring. It felt mechanical, like being measured for a dress she wasn't sure she'd ever wear.

"Dani," Sarah said at the end, voice softening, "I know this is a lot. If you're not ready, you can call and move or cancel. There's no pressure."

"Understood," Daniela said.

She hung up and sat very still.

For a few minutes, she let her mind go blank.

Then, inevitably, pictures seeped in.

The donor. A stranger. Somewhere out there, someone whose own grief or history had pushed them into filling out a form and saying, 'I want to help a couple like them'.

The widow in Aspley. Given she refused to let one terrible day be the full stop on Michael's journey. On their journey.

Now the clinic picks them, out of all the possible people they may have selected, to be at the front of the queue.

The phone rang again. She let it go to the machine this time.

Her mother-in-law's warm voice kicked in.

"Hi love, just calling to see how you and Michael are. No rush to call back. I'll drop some food around later anyway. Hope you're well. Happy … well, you know. Thinking of you."

'Happy what?' Daniela thought. Happy still-not-parents? Happy pretending with a dog?

This was not what she'd planned. Not what she'd dreamed.

This was something else. But it was something at least.

And, sitting there in the quiet with her own thoughts, maybe, just maybe, that something could still be perfect.

CHAPTER 21

WHAT REALLY MATTERS

Brisbane, late 1995

Michael stood in the hallway and bent down to slip off his work boots.

Daniela's voice came from the kitchen.

"You might as well leave your shoes on," she called.

He exhaled, slid his feet back into his boots and walked down the hall.

Daniela sat at the table, elbows on the laminate, hands clasped. In front of her lay a folded piece of paper with the clinic's letterhead peeking out. The words Brisbane Fertility Centre might as well have been in neon.

She looked tired. More than a standard end-of-shift tired.

"Hi," he said.

"Hi," she replied.

He hovered at the edge of the room.

"Mum says hello," he offered. "She sent food. It's in the car. Enough lasagne to feed the Queensland State of Origin team."

"Of course she did." A faint crease touched the corner of her mouth, then left. "You can bring it in later."

He nodded, throat dry.

"Do you want me to …?" He gestured awkwardly at the chair opposite.

"Sit," she said. "Please."

He sat.

For a moment they just breathed, looking at the paper between them in awkward silence.

"I had an appointment," she said at last, touching the corner of the page. "About the donor program."

He swallowed.

"And?" he asked.

"They explained things," she said. "Success rates. Legal stuff. What it means for the children in the future. What it means for the parents also."

She gave a half-attempted smile.

"They even had diagrams," she went on. "You'd have loved the diagrams. Very thorough."

He tried to smile, failed.

"Do you … want to do it?" he asked.

She looked at him properly then, really looked, like she had that morning at the café, only without as much raw shock.

"I don't know," she said. "I know I don't want to spend the rest of my life wondering if there was one more thing we could have tried. I know I don't want to do it alone."

A pause.

"And I know," she added quietly, "that I still haven't worked out how to keep both versions of you in my head at once, the man who walked into that TAB with a fake shotgun, and the man who cried in Dr Jonze's office when he said he had nothing left to give."

"I'm trying to help this process," he said. "By being the second more than the first."

"I know," she said. "Some days I can see it. Some days I can't."

He reached across the table, then checked himself.

"Can I …?" he asked.

She hesitated, then turned her hand palm up.

He took it. Her fingers felt cool. Familiar, but different.

"I'm scared," he admitted. "Of doing this donor thing. Of messing it up. Of watching you go through treatment again and not being able to fix or control the outcome. Of looking at a child one day and seeing all the ways I'm not them."

"Me too," she said. But I think I'm more fearful of sitting in this house at fifty and thinking we walked away from the last chance because we were too proud or too tired."

He nodded.

"So, we do it scared," he said.

"So, we do it scared, together," she reaffirmed.

They sat there a while longer, hands joined over the cheap table, not rushing to flick through all the paperwork, just happy to be in each other's presence again.

"Right," Daniela said, sounding more like herself than she had in months. "You should bring that lasagne in before it gets stolen by some hungry pack of Mt Gravatt High school kids wandering the streets. Plus, I need to eat well to ensure my body is ready to grow a little human soon."

He stood, light-headed.

He carried the lasagne in from the car, the dish warm through the tea towel.

They ate at the same table where the harsh words had previously been exchanged. They talked about small things; his mum's habit of over-catering, her colleague's upcoming wedding, the neighbour's new dog that barked at possums.

Now, for the first time since he'd walked into that TAB with a fake shotgun under his arm, Michael felt like he was again heading in the right direction.

Not towards some ideal of society's macho version of success. Towards the woman down the hall. Towards the life they still might build together, however it turned out. Towards the much harder work of staying true to his authentic, kind self; the best version of Michael Whelan.

Later, when he lay in bed next to Daniela again, he realised he wasn't rehearsing lies for the future. He was rehearsing answers. Honest ones. The only ones that now mattered.

CHAPTER 22

CONNECTION

Sydney, late 1995

The taxi slid through late-afternoon traffic, past stained terraces and balconies sagging under furniture. The city air had that Sydney mix of smog and self-importance.

Daniela watched it move by. Beside her, Michael picked at a loose thread on his trouser leg. His worried gaze fixed on the windscreen, like the driver was taking them back to the examination room where someone would mark their performance in red pen.

Their thighs touched when the cab lurched. She shifted her hand across until her fingers brushed his. He retracted, then let his hand rest over hers. His palm was damp.

"You'll be alright," she said quietly. "We both will."

He gave a thin nod without taking his eyes off the road.

They'd flown down that morning. The plane's climb out of Brisbane had felt, for Daniela, like choosing again; to stay, to try, to risk. He'd stared out the window at the disappearing suburbs, hands clasped on the armrests, and she'd known he was processing more than clouds.

Hazel's letter had been blunt about it: this money won't clean you; it just buys you better choices. Daniela had read that line several times. Better choices. This trip to Sydney was one of them.

The cab pulled up outside a narrow terrace in Darlinghurst. The sign by the buzzer read *Fertility & Family Clinic* in frosted lettering. Someone had tried to soften the place with pot plants by the stairs. It looked less like a hospital, more like a boutique law firm for people who could afford good problems.

Daniela paid, thanked the driver. Michael stood on the footpath, staring at the doorway as if there might be a sign saying, 'no *armed robbers or their wives beyond this point*'.

"You ready?" she asked.

"No," he said. "But I'm here."

"That'll do," she said. "For now."

Inside, the clinic was all pale wood and muted colours. No harsh fluorescents, no antiseptic smell. Just the faint scent of eucalyptus and someone's perfume.

The receptionist smiled the way people were taught to smile in training videos.

"Hi there. Michael and Daniela?"

"That's us," Daniela said.

"Great. You're here for the donor information session with Agnes?"

"Yes."

"If you'd like to take a seat, she'll be out in a moment."

They sat on a soft couch near a low table scattered with magazines. Baby photos, of course.

"Remember when we thought we'd send one of those?" Michael murmured, nodding at the table.

"Still might," she said.

A door opened down the hall.

"Michael and Daniela?" a woman called.

She was in her fifties, hair pulled back, glasses on a chain. Soft cardigan, sensible shoes. Not the white-coat authority of Dr Jonze back in Brisbane, but something steadier, less clinical.

"I'm Agnes," she said. "Come on through."

They followed her into a small meeting room. There were three chairs on one side of a low table, two on the other. Agnes sat in the middle of the three, invited them to the other side.

"I'm a counsellor with the clinic," she said. "Today isn't about signing anything. It's just talking. Giving you information. Seeing how it sits."

"We thought we'd be doing all this with … our own stuff," Michael blurted. "You know. My … contribution."

Agnes nodded.

"I've read your file," she said. "I'm sorry it's been such a long road. You've done more failed rounds than most couples manage. That's a lot of grief for two people to carry."

Daniela swallowed. Her throat felt thick.

"Today," Agnes went on, "we'll talk a bit about what it means to use a donor. Legally, medically, emotionally."

"Before we get into it, I'd like to ask you both one thing. It's a nosy question, but it matters," Agnes said.

"Go on," Daniela said.

"When you imagine a child, what's the part that hurts most about this not being straightforward? Is it the cost? The loss of a genetic connection? The unfairness? Or something else?"

Silence stretched.

"For me," Daniela said slowly, "it's … watching everyone else have it easy. Just deciding and then … it happens. No charts, no invoices. No needles."

"And the genetics?" she asked gently.

Daniela glanced at Michael.

"I wanted a child who was … ours," she said. "The whole

old-fashioned way. Your mum saying, 'They've got your eyes, and his complexion'."

Michael watched the floor.

"For me," he said, voice low, "it's walking around knowing I'm the reason. That there's nothing in me to pass on. And worrying that every time the child laughs in a way that isn't mine, I'll see it as a reminder of what I couldn't do."

Agnes nodded, as if she'd heard versions of this multiple times previously but still cared enough to acknowledge like it was the first.

"I've got some reading for you," she said. "Legal, medical, all the fun bits. There's no rush. Whatever you decide has to belong to you, not the clinic."

Michael looked at the folder, then at Agnes, then at Daniela. For once, the urge to apologise for existing wasn't louder than everything else.

"What happens," he asked, "if we … do decide to go ahead?"

Agnes folded her hands.

"Then we provide you with further information regarding the donor who has come forward to assist your journey to parenthood."

"If you're comfortable after that, the next step is to meet with me again, and the donor in person."

Daniela felt Michael's fingers tighten around hers.

"And we can start that … when?" she asked.

"He actually lives in Sydney, so we would reach out and see if we can arrange the meeting while you're already in town. Could be a challenge to align calendars, but worth a try."

Michael let out a slow breath.

"I don't know if I'll ever feel ready," he said. "But I know I don't want to go back to Brisbane having just … hovered on the edge again."

He turned to Daniela.

"If we come back again in the next few days to meet him, that doesn't mean we're promising anything. It just means we're walking through the next door, together, I guess."

"I'm intrigued, but afraid," she said. "But I agree, I don't want to head home with nothing new to hope for."

She looked at Agnes.

"If you can book that meeting as discussed," she said, voice steadier than she felt, "we'd like to move forward. At least to that."

"Alright," she said. "Leave it with me."

As they stepped outside, they couldn't wait any longer. Michael ripped opened the envelope to learn more about the stranger who might help start their family.

***

Three days later, they walked back up the same narrow steps to the clinic.

Michael was carrying a small paper bag from a bookshop near the station. His palm had left a damp patch on the side of it.

Agnes was waiting just inside the glass door.

"Michael, Daniela," she said. "Good to see you again. Our donor and his family are already here. Come through."

She led them down the short hallway and opened the door to a small meeting room.

Inside, someone had laid a play mat on the floor. A little boy in a striped T-shirt sat cross-legged on it, rolling two toy cars back and forth, making a low engine noise under his breath.

The man and woman with him looked up as Agnes ushered Michael and Daniela in.

"This is Paul and Gloria," Agnes said. "And Jack."

Jack glanced up, took a quick glance at the newcomers, then went back to his cars.

Paul was mid-thirties, maybe a couple of years older than Michael, with dark hair going soft at the temples. Sleeves rolled, forearms tanned. Gloria had her hair pulled back in a loose knot, a cotton dress, tiredness around her eyes like any parent with young children.

They all shuffled hands and hellos, finding places around the low table while Jack stayed in his little world on the mat.

Michael cleared his throat, lifting the bag a little.

"Um … we weren't sure what the etiquette is for something like this," he said. "But Agnes mentioned Jack would be here, so we brought … this. Just to say thank you. For meeting us."

Gloria's face softened as she took the bag.

"Oh, that's very kind," she said. "You didn't have to."

She peered inside and smiled. There was a small board book about trucks and a new matchbox car still in its packet.

"Jack," she said gently. "Can you say thank you?"

Jack glanced over, eyed the shiny car, and shuffled across on his knees to accept it.

"Fank you," he mumbled, already working at the cardboard.

Michael's shoulders dropped a millimetre. The room felt less like an interview, more like someone's slightly awkward lounge room.

Agnes sat in her usual spot in the middle of the three chairs, with Michael and Daniela on one side of the table, Paul and Gloria on the other.

"Alright," she said. "I know this is a strange situation for everyone. So, I want to acknowledge that up-front. Most people don't grow up imagining they'll sit in a room like this, talking about making a baby with strangers while a toddler does burnouts on the carpet."

Jack obligingly revved his new car along the skirting board.

A small, shaky laugh went around the group.

"Today is about two things," Agnes continued. "First, to walk through what this process looks like when the donor is identifiable and open to contact. Second, for you to hear from each other. Why you're here. What you need to feel okay going ahead. There's no pressure to decide everything by the end of this hour, but it's a chance to see if this feels like a fit."

She glanced at Paul.

"Paul's completed all the medical and psychological screening," she said. "He's been approved by the clinic. This would be his first donation. He's also made it clear he wishes to donate to one family only."

Paul nodded, fingers linked together between his knees.

"I'm not ... I don't want to be some kind of faceless factory," he said. "No offence to anyone who does that, but that's not what I'm here for."

Michael swallowed. There was something in the bluntness that felt familiar.

Agnes turned to Daniela and Michael.

"Why don't we start with you both," she said. "Just a short version of what's brought you here and what matters most for you in a donor arrangement."

Daniela drew in a breath.

"We've been at this a long time," she said. "Years of IVF. We kept being the couple in the waiting room who'd tried the thing that didn't work."

She glanced at Michael, then at Jack, now lining his cars in a neat row.

"And at a certain point," she went on, "it stopped feeling like we were making choices and more like things were just being taken off us. Options. Time. Money. Our bodies. Michael's especially."

Michael stared at his hands.

"I used to be the guy who fixed things," he said quietly. "Engineer, right? You give me a broken system; I'll find the fault. Then I became the fault. You see the numbers and hear the dreaded word infertile and you eventually need to accept there's nothing you can tighten or replace or fix this situation."

He risked a quick look at Paul.

"I didn't come to this easily," he said. "The idea of using someone else's sperm. It felt like … handing my place over. But sitting in the dark with Dani after another failed cycle, it started to feel more like someone had already taken that place away and I was just pretending otherwise."

Daniela nodded.

"What matters to us," she said, "is that if we do this, our child doesn't grow up with a blank space where half their story should be. We don't want a 'donor number'. We want a person they can know about. Maybe meet, if everyone's comfortable, when they're old enough. We think that's important for their mental health, their sense of who they are."

Her voice caught a little.

"We're not trying to replace a father," she added quickly, glancing at Michael. "Michael will be their dad. That's not in question. But we don't want to pretend biology doesn't exist either."

Paul listened, jaw working, eyes flicking down to Jack and back again.

Agnes let the silence sit for a beat, then turned to him.

"Paul," she said gently. "Can you talk a bit about why you wanted to donate? And what you imagine contact looking like, if Michael and Daniela decide to go ahead?"

He nodded slowly, as if he'd rehearsed this in his head on the way over and still wasn't sure he'd get it right.

"Yeah," he said. "Look, the short version is … my brother never got the chance."

He rubbed a thumb along the edge of his watch.

"His name was Luke," he said. "Younger than me. Funny bugger. He was the one who was going to have the big noisy family. He loved kids. Always the uncle rolling on the floor with them, you know?"

He swallowed.

"Then when he was twenty-eight, he got leukaemia. They blasted him with chemo. Saved his life for a while, but it took his fertility. Doctors were very matter-of-fact about it, like it was just another side-effect on the list. Nausea, hair loss, can't ever have kids."

He looked down to compose himself.

"I watched him try to make peace with that," he went on. "Watched him sit in a waiting room like this with his girlfriend while some specialist explained what they couldn't do. And then, in the end, he passed away faster than anyone could have predicted. No kids. No physical legacy running around, just photos and the stories we tell."

Gloria's fingers slipped over his wrist. He let them sit there.

"After he died," Paul said, "I kept thinking how unfair it was that something completely out of his control stole that from him. And then I'd see couples on TV ads, or in the park, or mates with babies, and I'd … I don't know. I'd feel this urge to do something other than just be sad and angry on his behalf."

He took a breath.

"When I saw an article about identifiable donors in a clinic like this, it clicked," he said. "I thought … I've got what Luke lost. I'm not using it much beyond this little bloke here. And maybe a sibling in the future" He nodded at Jack, who was now carefully driving his new car over a chair leg. "If I can tip the scales back in the favour of someone else, maybe that's one small positive outcome to come from Luke's cruel story."

He met Michael's eyes.

"I don't see it as giving away a child," he said. "I see it as giving you a chance to have one. Your family. Your joy. I'm not looking to have a dozen kids out there. I told the clinic I want to donate to one couple, one family, and then that's it. I want to know, if this works, that I played a part in helping a couple who had been presented with challenges to conceive through no fault of their own."

Daniela felt something in her chest loosen.

"And the contact?" she asked carefully. "What does that look like, for you?"

Paul sat back a fraction, considering.

"I don't want to be a ghost," he said. "I'm happy for my name and basic details to be available from the start. Photos if you want them. If you decide to tell your child early, which, personally I think is healthier, I'd be honoured if they grew up knowing there's this bloke called Paul who helped at the beginning."

He glanced at Gloria.

"We've talked about it a lot," he said. "If, when they're older, they want to meet, I'm open to that. A coffee, a walk, answering questions. I certainly don't plan on turning up at your place with Christmas presents every year unless that's something we all talk about and all agree on. I'm not looking to co-parent. I already have enough on my plate with young Jack here. But I'm not hiding either."

Gloria spoke for the first time.

"Like Paul said, Michael is their dad and you are their mum Daniela," she said, meeting Daniela's eyes. "That's really important. We've got Jack, and I know how it would feel if someone blurred those lines for him. But I also know how it would mess with my own head if I knew there was someone out there connected to me, and everyone had to pretend they didn't exist. This way, it's honest, solidly honest."

Daniela let out a relieved breath.

"That's what we want," she said. "Honest. Not some big reveal when they're fifteen and already dealing with exams and hormones. Just … the truth, when the time is right."

Agnes nodded.

"So we're hearing that identifiable information from birth is acceptable to everyone," she said. "Ongoing updates, photos, letters, perhaps a yearly summary would be negotiable between you. And potential face-to-face contact when the child is older, if all parties agree."

She glanced around the group. No one flinched.

"Legally," she added, "Paul would have no parental rights or responsibilities. That doesn't change, even if you know each other socially. Michael is the legal father. That's written into the law and into the clinic's consent forms."

Michael's shoulders straightened a little at that.

"I need you to hear me say it out loud," he said, looking first at Paul, then at Gloria. "If this works … I'll be their dad. Every school concert, every midnight vomit, every argument about curfews. That's mine. I'm not asking you to share that. I just … I don't want them growing up with a question mark they can never chase down."

Paul nodded.

"I get it," he said. "Luke used to say the worst part wasn't knowing he might die. It was not knowing what would be left of him if he did. You're trying to make sure your child doesn't have that kind of question mark. That makes sense to me."

Jack drove his car into the leg of Michael's chair with a soft thunk and looked up at him as if noticing him properly for the first time.

"Crash," he announced.

Michael gave a startled little laugh.

"Yeah," he said. "Big crash."

He looked at Daniela. Her eyes were shining, but there was a steadiness there he hadn't seen in a long time.

Agnes let the room breathe for a few moments, then spoke.

"Are there any deal-breakers we haven't touched on?" she asked. "Anything that keeps you awake at three in the morning when you picture this?"

Daniela thought of all the nights she'd lain awake anyway, picturing nothing happening at all.

"I'm mostly scared of regret," she said. "Regretting not doing this now, especially after meeting you and hearing your touching story."

Michael turned to Paul.

"I hate that your brother went through what he did," he said. "I hate that this is how our stories overlap. But I'm grateful you're here. I don't know how else to say it without sounding like a Hallmark card."

Paul's mouth twisted.

"'Grateful' works," he said. "I'm grateful you're here too. I'd feel like a bit of a dick if I'd gone through all those tests and there was no one on the other end."

Agnes smiled.

"Alright," she said gently. "I'm going to ask a very simple, very big question. Michael and Daniela, based on what you've heard today, do you want to proceed with Paul as your donor? We can take it one consent form at a time, but I need to know whether this feels like a 'yes', a 'no', or a 'not yet'."

Daniela looked at Michael. For a second she saw them back at the start; cheap suits, nervous smiles, the two of them in a park talking about future kids like it was as simple as picking baby names from a list.

"I think it's a 'yes'," she said, voice rough.

Michael's hand found hers.

"Yeah," he said. "If you're still willing, Paul … it's a 'yes' from me."

Paul let out a deep breath.

"I'm willing," he said. "One family. Your family. Let's give it a crack."

Gloria squeezed his arm.

Agnes made a brief note on the file and then closed it, respecting the moment.

Daniela looked at Jack and pictured Luke, a man gone too soon, whose absence had nudged another generous man into this room.

This, she thought, finally felt like choosing, instead of being chosen for.

CHAPTER 23

NEW LIFE

Brisbane, early 1997

J ust over four years had passed since Claire hit the floor of the Aspley TAB, but the memory sat waiting for the wrong sound or name to welcome it in.

Most days, it didn't. Most days, the Royal Brisbane Hospital was loud enough to drown it out; monitors, crying kids, parents asking the same question ten different ways.

In the staff cafeteria, Claire sat in the corner, staring into bad coffee. The smell of reheated curry in the microwave hung in the air. The lighting made everyone look tired, exhausted.

A tray landed opposite her. Jane dropped into the seat, ponytail crooked, mascara smudged.

"Shift your homework," Jane said, nudging a folded Australian Nursing Journal out of the way. "I need room for my chips and my midlife crisis."

"Rough morning?" Claire enquired.

"Three febrile kids, one parent who thinks Panadol is part of the government's conspiracy plot, and a Registrar who talks to me like I'm his mother's cleaner. So … fine."

"Please. You're terrifying when you're annoyed," Claire said, shoving a chip in her mouth. "You'll work it out."

"How's your lot on the ward?" Jane returned her interest.

"Clinging on," Claire said. "Kids are doing better than the parents. I'm pretending to be calm while internally screaming."

"If that's you screaming, I'd hate to see actual," Jane said. "You hold that ward together with spit and tape."

Compliments still sat on Claire like clothes a size too big. She shrugged and reached for her coffee.

"It's just the job," she said.

Before Jane could argue, a shadow fell across the table.

Tony from theatres stood there, tray in hand, hair damp from a scrub. He had that restless, unbridled energy that made older nurses bet on whether he'd burn out or end up running the place.

"Mind if I sit?" he asked, eyes flicking to Claire and away again.

"Go on," Jane said, already smirking. "You can help me entice Claire to come out with us for a dance in the Valley one evening after work."

Tony dropped into the chair beside her. The vinyl squeaked.

"I've been meaning to say 'hello' properly," he said to Claire, unwrapping a salad roll. "You're Claire, right? Legendary peds nurse?"

Claire raised an eyebrow. "Legendary's a bit much. Must be a slow news day."

Once, the badge on her chest had said Dr Claire Sutherland. Losing that, the investigation, had felt like an amputation. When the Trimax money cleared, she'd paid for rehab, set up the charitable fund, and the first term of a nursing degree.

Now, somehow, the ward called her 'legendary' instead of 'dangerous'.

"Not what I've heard," Tony said. "Apparently if you ever retire, peds collapses within a week."

"Told you," Jane murmured.

Heat crept up Claire's neck. She looked down at the coffee.

"I'm just doing my job," she said, reflex kicking in.

Tony shrugged. "Plenty of people 'just do their job' and still manage to stuff it up. You don't."

The bluntness knocked her off balance. Nearly eight years of meetings in community halls had taught her to let the odd bit of praise land without smashing it to pieces. On good days, anyway.

"How's the ward?" Tony asked, taking a bite. "Heard about your girl in bed 6."

"Post-op," Jane said. "Parents with degrees from the back of a cornflakes box?"

Claire rolled her eyes. Tony smiled at her.

Jane checked her watch and groaned.

"Team meeting in ten," she said. "If I'm late, one of the consultants will make me explain 'quality of life' using pie charts to the group."

She drained her coffee and stood.

Jane flashed a peace sign and vanished into the noise.

Tony glanced at his pager.

"I should head back also," he said. "Nice to finally talk properly."

"You too," Claire said.

He hesitated.

"A few of us are going to Ric's Café on Friday," he added. "Staff drinks. Nothing wild. If you feel like it … you'd be welcome."

"It's a lovely offer Tony, but these days my wild nights are made up of instant coffee and Tim Tams. I'm a real Rager." Sarcasm evident in her voice.

Understanding moved across his face.

"Right," he said. "I heard you don't drink."

"Not if I want to keep my life," she said. "But thanks for the invite. Really."

"Another time," he said. "We'll do the hardcore hospital thing and complain about rostering instead."

She allowed herself a small smile.

"That I can do," she said.

His pager beeped.

"That's me," he said, standing. "See you on the ward, Claire."

She watched him go, then finished the now-lukewarm coffee anyway.

'He's alright', she told herself as she felt the buzz against her hip.

LABOUR WARD — ASSIST. SHORT-STAFFED.

She frowned. Maternity wasn't her usual patch.

Claire binned her cup and headed for the lifts.

The lift dragged its way up the shaft and eventually opened to the quieter environment of postnatal. Softer lights. Softer voices. The cries of little lungs testing themselves out.

A midwife at the desk waved her over. "Claire, sorry, can you do a quick review for me? We're under the pump. Bed twelve, basic newborn check."

"Sure," Claire said.

The chart sat in its plastic holder outside the room. She flipped it open.

WHELAN, BERNADETTE — GIRL.

Her eyes snagged on the surname, Whelan.

Could be anyone, she told herself. Brisbane was no longer a country town.

She pushed the door open.

Inside, a woman lay propped up in the bed, hair scraped back, gown sliding off one shoulder. A baby in a pink wrap was tucked into her arm nook. Beside her, fussing with the drip stand stood a man in a crumpled shirt.

He turned his head.

Michael Whelan.

Older, softer around the middle, a touch less hair. But it was him. The man with the fake shotgun in Hazel's TAB. The man whose hands had shaken so badly she'd watched the barrel and waited for physics to take over.

Her body remembered the day her blood pressure dropped before her mind could catch up.

"Hi," she said, her voice somehow steady. "I'm Claire, one of the nurses. Just here to check on your little one, if that's okay."

The woman looked up, "Of course. This is Bernadette."

Claire stepped closer, letting the baby take over her field of vision. Safer that way. Small screwed-up face, damp wisps of dark hair, fists folded like she was ready for a fight with gravity.

She slid the stethoscope into her ears and focused on the simple, grounding stuff: heart sounds, chest rise, skin colour, tone. Bernadette wriggled once in protest, then settled.

"How is she?" the woman asked.

"She's good," Claire said. "Strong cry, lungs sound clear. Everything looks right on track."

The woman sagged a little into the pillows. "That's … that's good. Sorry, I'm Daniela. This is Michael."

"Hi," Michael said quietly.

Claire looked directly towards him. His eyes were firmly fixed on the baby, not on her. No flicker of recognition. Of course there wasn't. That day in the TAB, she'd been one pale stranger on the wrong end of his plan.

Still, the sight of him standing here in a visitor's band made something in her chest twist.

"Any feeding trouble? Settling okay?" she asked, going back to the checklist.

"We're still working it out," Daniela said. "The midwives say we're doing fine, but it feels like we're improvising."

"That's normal," Claire said. "Nobody feels like they know what they're doing at the start. You learn from each other."

She made a couple of notes on the chart. It gave her hands somewhere to go while her brain held two versions of the same man side by side.

"Thank you," he said, finally looking up at her. "For checking on her."

"It's my job," Claire replied.

She closed the chart. "Your midwife will pop back in to go through feeding and monitoring. If you need anything, just press the buzzer. Congratulations, she really is beautiful."

In the corridor, Claire walked until she found the stairwell, pushed through the heavy door and let it clunk shut behind her.

Concrete walls. A strip of harsh light. The faint smell of disinfectant. No babies. No Whelan.

She leaned against the cool rail and let herself breathe properly for the first time since she'd seen the name on the chart.

Of all the babies in all the wards, she thought. Of all the fathers.

One bad afternoon stretched four years and all the way to this floor.

A short, humourless laugh caught in her throat. "Of course it's you," she said softly to the empty stairwell.

Her pager buzzed. Paediatrics. Life going on, messily, at its usual pace.

Claire straightened, wiped a hand over her face, and opened the stairwell door.

As she re-entered the corridor, she couldn't help but focus her thoughts on baby Bernadette; born into the long shadow of a fixed horse race in the desert, and a sacred pact made in suburbia.

CHAPTER 24

GOOD COMPANY

Alice Springs, late 2026

Nothing escaped from the summer heat of Alice Springs, not even the truth.

More than three decades had slipped by since the race at Alice Springs and the robbery in Aspley, but the past still walked beside Angus in the dust.

He still remembered the week after Trimax came in – the seventh at Alice Springs.

Mac's voice, usually all swagger and jokes, had gone quiet in the way Angus knew meant real trouble.

While they had baptised the win a miracle, it never quite washed everyone clean.

Word got around. A junior bookie lost his job. A jockey in the Territory suddenly wasn't getting the good rides. A couple of small-time punters found themselves politely uninvited from certain pubs. Angus slept with one eye open for months, waiting for a knock on the door that never came.

In the end, the knock did come. Not from anyone in a suit, and not about Trimax. Another job gone sideways, a debt collected the ugly way, his name turning up in the wrong notebook. They called it 'handling stolen property' and 'aggravated assault'.

One week he was still a familiar face around Brisbane pubs and TABs, the next he was just a story Hazel might hear third-hand: Angus did a stint. Then he was gone.

Angus felt the oppressive heat pressing on his skin as he shuffled along the footpath, each step a small complaint from his joints. His chest rose and fell in short, irritated huffs. Every breath scraped his lungs with dust, and every exhale felt like it could be his last.

He was eighty, maybe. He'd stopped counting birthdays after the last stretch inside. Some days, he told himself he'd earned this ending, a slow fade in a town that barely knew his name. Other days, he wanted to scream at the sky: "Why this way? Why so slow?"

When they finally let him out after that last stint, Brisbane had felt too small and too full of past indiscretions. He'd tried Darwin for a while, cash work on doors and truck yards, too much beer, not enough sleep. He then followed a mate inland chasing 'easier money' and cheaper rent. Alice stuck. Nobody here knew enough of his history to cross the street when they saw him coming.

The main pub in Alice Springs glowed ahead, a dull yellow rectangle in the early evening. He remembered when places like this had been full of blokes he wanted to forget. There were still some he remembered; men who'd shouted him drinks, men who'd hired him to do things nobody wrote down, men whose names he only ever knew as nicknames. Behind each one there were broken things that didn't always heal. Teeth. Windows. Nerves.

The older he got, the heavier that ledger felt.

He'd never put much stock in heaven or hell, but lately he'd started to wonder what, if anything, could help square up a lopsided ledger like his.

Ben, the young man behind the bar, looked up, cloth in hand. "Holey dooley. Thought you'd finally given up on us, Gus."

Angus slid onto a stool, bones groaning. "Not yet." He tapped the bar with two fingers. "Whisky. Make it a big one."

The glass landed in front of him, golden and trembling. He held it up, watching the liquid catch the low light. "Careful, son," he said. "You keep filling me up like this, and I'll start thinking you care."

"Maybe I do." Ben grinned, leaning forward. "Maybe I just like the stories."

"Stories," Angus muttered, knocking back the first whiskey. It burned a path down his throat, sharp as truth. "Aye. That's one word for it."

The second glass came slower, poured while they talked about nothing, footy scores, the weather that refused to break. But Angus could feel Ben's eyes on him, could sense the lad's curiosity building.

"You're looking crook," Ben finally said.

"Doctor says I'm riddled." Angus tapped his chest. "Lungs. Liver. All the soft bits. Like weeds in a garden. Can't keep up with the pulling."

Ben's face seemed to drop. "Sorry, mate."

"Don't be." Angus sipped instead of swallowing. "Could've been a bullet. Could've been a knife. Instead, I get the drawn-out curtain call. A mercy, really."

Silence hung between them. The jukebox muttered a country ballad no one listened to. Pool balls cracked in the back corner.

The third whiskey came. Angus turned the glass in his hand, thumb running circles on the rim. "You ever think about the end, Ben? About what comes after?"

Ben shifted, looking cautious. "Sometimes."

"I think about it all the time." Angus's voice dropped. "I'll tell you what scares me. Not hell, not fire and brimstone. Just the dark. The empty nothing. Me, alone in it, with every ghost I created."

Ben's gaze held momentarily. "Ghosts?"

"Aye." Angus let the word linger. He closed his eyes. The bloke in Brisbane who never walked right again after a message job went too far. The corner-store owner who paid 'insurance' for three winters straight because Angus stood in his doorway every Friday night, smiling like it was just business. The young fella inside who'd taken the blame for a job Angus had planned, and who never got the chance to be anything but somebody's cautionary tale.

"They're all there," he said, opening his eyes again. "Every bloody one of them. And when the dark comes, it'll just be me and them. No jury, no judge. Just me replaying it until the black swallows me whole."

Ben poured a fourth drink, slower than the others. "Maybe you don't have to face them alone. Maybe saying it out loud, here, now, makes it easier to carry."

Angus barked a laugh, though it caught in his throat and turned into a cough. "You think confession turns a man clean? I've done more wrong than a priest's ears could stand."

"Maybe," Ben said. "But maybe it's not about them. Maybe it's about you forgiving yourself before it's too late."

Angus stared at him, really stared. The boy had no right to sound so wise. But he did. And for the first time, Angus felt the heaviness ease from his hand.

He raised it, drained it, and tapped it back onto the bar. "Maybe you're right, son. Or maybe you're just too young to know better."

Ben didn't answer. He just poured another and set it down gently, as if offering something more than whisky.

The kid looked at him with something Angus hadn't expected; kindness. "You scared?"

The question hung in the air. Angus tried to scoff, but it came out as a cracked voice. "Bloody terrified. Never thought I'd admit that. I spent a lifetime pretending I wasn't scared of anything, cops, jails, enemies, dying young. But now …" He stared into his glass. "It's like looking into a pit. No rope, no ladder."

"Have you talked to someone about it?"

"Who would want to listen to me?"

Ben replied, "There's a new clinic that just opened. Bulk billing. Psychologists. It's for people living here who can't afford Sydney prices. They aim to give everyone a chance at … well, I don't know, peace."

Angus rolled the word around in his mind. Peace. It felt foreign to him, and he chuckled.

"You really think some therapist is going to forgive me for the lives I've messed up?" For the years he'd taken envelopes and looked the other way, when fear did the talking for people who couldn't afford to say 'no'.

"Not forgiveness from others, mate. Maybe, help you forgive yourself." Ben offered in a caring tone.

Angus shuffled along the street, the sun beating down on the red dust. His walking stick tapped rhythmically against the ground, matching his laboured breaths.

The clinic appeared unremarkable: a weatherboard cottage, pale against the ochre earth. A plaque by the door read:

Mental Health Support. Accessible Care for All Communities. Funded by an Anonymous Donor Family.

Inside, the waiting room was modest. Plastic chairs, a shelf of dog-eared books, and a painting of gum trees adorned the walls. At the reception desk, a framed note in neat handwriting read:

"This clinic exists because no one should be left behind. Especially in places where too much has already been taken."

Taken. The word cut into him.

"Mr Stenhouse?"

He looked up to see a young woman in the doorway. She had blue eyes and a calm demeanour, offering a gentle smile.

"Come through."

He followed her and lowered himself into a chair across from her. The room had a faint eucalyptus scent.

"There is a glass of water there for you if you want it, on the table there."

"Now, before we get started formally today, Mr Stenhouse, given your pre-visit form indicates this is your first visit to a psychologist's clinic, are there any questions you'd like to ask?"

"You don't have to, of course," she clarified. "Just anything, even generally, that may ease you into our session today."

He studied her, feeling an unexplained tug of familiarity, her hair catching the light, her calming voice.

"Who set this place up?" he asked.

She hesitated, then flashed a sly smile. "Well, if I told you that Mr Stenhouse, I'm afraid I would then have to kill you."

For the first time in weeks, Angus laughed, a deep, rattling laugh that shook his entire frame.

But when he looked down to return to himself, to more serious matters, he noticed the name tag clipped to her blouse:

BERNADETTE WHELAN.

The name struck him. He froze, air catching in his throat. Whelan. The robbery. Michael. The winnings 'taken' by questionable means. And now this, a clinic built on generosity and giving back.

The pieces fell into place with startling clarity, and something softened within him.

If this was where the line ended, perhaps he wasn't walking into the dark alone after all.

Maybe, by some strange twist of fate, he'd ended up in good company.

Thank You

Rhianne and Mary, Dad, Matt, Ian Mathieson, Cholm Johnson, Ian Hanrahan, Paul Gordon, Ben Richardson, Stuart Skerman, Jess Chaplin, Faber Writing a Novel Class of 2023.

Peter Bell is a Brisbane storyteller. His first book, *Stepping Out the Other Side – finding purpose through adversity*, received a Gold Award from the Nonfiction Authors Association in 2021. *Stepping Out* explores Pete's mental health challenges and how he found stability and purpose through the process. He completed Faber Writing Academy's intensive Writing a Novel program in 2023. He is a highly regarded property analyst/business adviser and a strong advocate for breaking down the stigma associated with mental illness. He regularly shares his knowledge and personal mental health journey at charitable events, on podcasts and in the media.